MW00640464

ANGRY BETTY

A Kate Darby Novel

JAMIE LEE SCOTT

ANGRY BETTY

Copyright © 2019 by Jamie Lee Scott

All rights reserved. Except for use in any review, the reproduction or utilization of this work in whole or in part in any form by any electronic, mechanical or other means, now known or hereafter invented, including xerography, photocopying and recording, or in any information storage or retrieval system, is forbidden without the written permission of the publisher, Novels & Coffee.

This is a work of fiction. Names, characters, places and incidents are either the product of the author's imagination or are used fictitiously, and any resemblance to actual persons, living or dead, business establishments, events or locales is entirely coincidental.

Text copyright © 2019 Jamie Lee Scott, All Rights Reserved

ISBN: 978-1-942245-25-4 ebook

ISBN: 978-1-942245-26-1 paperback

Get Jamie's Newsletter

Want to be the first to read Jamie Lee Scott know about new releases, get advanced sneak peeks at new novels, and fun giveaways?
Subscribe to Jamie's newsletter for
EXCLUSIVE novella ebook
HOMICIDE, LIFE WITH NICK
So if you're not a newsletter subscriber, here's your chance.
This is open to international readers too.
*must be deliverable online
Click here to get the newsletter!

Email me. I'd love to hear from you
jamie@jamieleescott.com http://www.jamieleescott.com

Website: http://www.jamieleescott.com
Twitter http://www.twitter.com/authorjamie

Facebook Fan Page:
http://www.facebook.com/authorjamie
Be a part of the Clues Crew and get a sneak peek at
works in progress
and join the fun and giveaways.
https://www.facebook.com/groups/jamiescluecrew/
Want to be the first to read Jamie Lee Scott know about
new releases, get advanced sneak peeks at new novels,
and fun giveaways?

About the Kate Darby novels:

I've been wanting to write a series to highlight our men and women in blue for quite some time, and I even started with a series called Uncertain, but I realized the novellas didn't do the stories justice. Then the idea came to write a series set in East Texas, so I made up the small city of Peculiar, Texas, and set my story in a place with a small college and a beautiful lake.

The stories in this series have instances of real occurrences that happen to uniform cops on a regular basis. I tried to portrait the real world as much as possible, but gave myself artistic license to change details to fit the stories.

Yes, it's true that small towns don't have a full detective unit, and the officers are required to investigate major crimes. Sometimes they are assisted by other agencies, but many times the crimes are investigated by the local cops. These are the stories of the police officers of Peculiar, Texas.

As for the titles:

Each title in this police procedural/crime fiction series is a cop slang term, and I'll be using the terms in alphabetical order, so you'll know the order in which to read the books.

I really hope you enjoy this series as much as I've enjoyed writing it.

COP SLANG

Term: Angry Betty
Usually a high, crackhead, crazy, mad female, arms
flailing, screaming, swearing

Chapter 1

Corporal Kate Darby looked at the clock on the dashboard of her patrol car. 5:30 am. Half an hour until her shift ended. Her friend in the restaurant business liked to say a slow night meant last minute customers, whose order wouldn't be enough money for the extra time she'd have to pay her employees to wait on and wait for the customer to eat and leave. And those customers always stayed and stayed, even after half the lights in the restaurant were turned off.

Kate wouldn't mind having to work a few extra hours. It would give her an excuse to cancel her morning meeting, even the thought of the phone call she received made her stomach turn.

"Miss Darby?" the woman on the phone said.

"Yes, this is Kate Darby," she responded warily, thinking maybe it was a sales call, but it came from a local area code. Robocall, she was sure of it. Weren't they tapping into local numbers these days?

"This is Eva Bonnet with Lloyd, Norris & Taylor. I'm calling to inform you that your grandfather, Edwin Barrow, died two weeks ago, and his will is being read at Mr. Norris' office tomorrow morning at nine. Mr. Norris thinks it's important you be there."

"My grandfather?" Kate asked. *"Where are you calling from?"*

"As I said, Lloyd, Norris & Taylor." The sickening sweet in her tone was well trained.

Kate shook her head. *"No, I mean what city? Because I think you may have the wrong person. I don't have a grandfather. I was raised in the foster system."*

"Ma'am, you are the daughter of Amy Darby, right?" Sounding so patient, Kate thought she must have to deal with idiots all day. Kate dealt with idiots all day and she knew the tone.

"I am," Kate said. *"Wow, this is unreal. I haven't seen or heard from my mom since I was very young. I'm pretty sure she said my grandparents were dead. But again, I was pretty young. I may be remembering it wrong."*

"Will you be able to make it to the reading, Ms. Darby?"

Kate took down the address. She had a grandfather. All this time. She wondered how long he'd known about her, and why the hell he hadn't come forward when DHS had taken her from her mother.

Kate agreed to be at the attorney's office at nine, and immediately wondered what the old man looked like. Tall, wiry, with a thick head of white hair? Or maybe short and dumpy, with a bald, shiny head? Whatever he looked like, he'd known about her and done nothing to help her situation when she was a grandkid. Screw him. She didn't want or need anything from him. And to go sit in a stuffy attorney's office and listen as an old man's will was read made her skin crawl just at the thought of it.

But maybe her grandfather didn't have anything to offer. Look at the daughter they raised. What a peach. But he had to have something, since his attorney was Mr. Norris, one of the partners. Didn't the lesser clients get the associates, and the better ones got the partners?

The conversation and the thoughts of the meeting rolled through her head on a loop during her entire shift. Lucky for her, it was a slow crime night, and as she patrolled the streets, her stomach churned at the thought of knowing her grandfather had been nearby all her life, and he'd never tried to contact her. She wondered about her grandmother, would she be at the reading? Who else would be there?

Only fifteen minutes until six o'clock. Kate turned onto Sutter Street. A white Mercedes rolled through the stop sign, right in front of her. "Not smart, asshole," she said aloud, thinking *Who doesn't stop when there's a cop car to your right at a four-way stop?*

She lit the guy up, following him as she radioed dispatch. "229 headquarters, copy signal 18 HQ."

"Go ahead, 229."

Kate gave the license number, color, make, and model. "Stand by for stop, HQ."

"Standing by."

"229 HQ, stop is going to be at Mission and Sixth. Occupied by one."

Easy enough, she'd check the driver's license, issue a warning, and send the guy on his way. Clock out, nap, go to the meeting with the lawyer.

She turned on her spotlight, then hit the button on her chest camera and opened the door, getting out of her car. Stepping up behind the Mercedes and touching the left rear fender with her right hand, to leave her presence on the car, she took two strides forward and said, "Good morn—"

"Why are you harassing me?" A greasy looking male in his thirties cut her off, clearly unhappy to have been pulled over.

"If stopping you for a traffic violation is harassment, it's new to me. You rolled through that stop sign at the Sutter Street intersection."

"What the fuck? I didn't roll through nothing."

Great way to end the day. When she'd first started as a cop, she dreaded the confrontations, expecting them at every stop, being relieved when it didn't happen. Not everyone was an asshole, usually just the ones who habitually broke the law, and yet they were being targeted or harassed. She'd grown a thick skin over the years, but she had to admit, she never stopped a car without being aware it could go wrong.

"Okay, may I see your license and registration, please?" Kate's patience was worn thin from the twelve-hour shift.

The driver reached across to the glove box and

4

Kate's senses ramped up, but not fast enough. She stepped back just as the driver stomped on the gas pedal and burned rubber as he drove off.

As she ran back to her car, she said, "Dude, it's on," then pressed the button on her radio and said, "Vehicle running. West on Mission."

Adrenaline pumping hard through her veins, she jumped in her car, shut the door and was moving before she heard it close. Trying to keep up, but aware she was in a neighborhood, she radioed in again. "229, vehicle turned left on Cypress."

She slammed her steering wheel hard when she made the left on Cypress and the Mercedes was gone. "Shit."

She slowed her car and continued to look down side streets. On St. Claire, she saw a commotion and turned right. Halfway down the block were two patrol vehicles. Two officers stood on the corner, near the street sign, staring at the white Mercedes.

It looked a little different than it did when she pulled the driver over, because it was now wheels up with all the windows broken, and instead of being on the street, it had come to a stop in a shallow ditch.

Kate pulled her car to the side of the road and got out. Walking over to the other cops, she said, "Tell me you've got my driver somewhere."

"Nope. Never even saw him," Officer Williams said.

His casual attitude about losing the driver made her want to pull out her baton and smack him up beside

5

the head. There was a reason the jerk fled, not just to make the last half hour on her shift interesting.

Williams would be under her supervision when she made sergeant. She'd give him an attitude adjustment soon enough.

"How is that possible? I wasn't ten seconds behind him."

She knew that wasn't exactly the truth. She'd been maybe fifteen seconds behind him but had slowed when she lost sight of him on Cypress. He had close to a minute, maybe two, on her by then.

"That's an eternity in a car chase," Williams said. "I turned the corner in time to see the car flip, but I never saw the driver. By the time I got to the car, he was gone. He can't be too far."

She walked to the Mercedes, looking closely for any signs of the driver and saw the trunk had popped open. Was he hiding in the trunk? Sounded like a stupid idea, but most criminals weren't exactly brain trusts. Stepping down into the ditch, she pulled out her flashlight and shown it into the darkness. "Holy shit."

Once again, she pressed the button on her radio. "Suspect fled. Possible 27 in the trunk. Call out a detective."

Twenty-seven, the code for a dead body. The way the car had landed in the ditch jammed the rear quarter panel and popped the trunk, but the ground kept it from opening far enough for the body to fall out. No way to get to the body until the wrecker came to pull the car out and turn it over. She didn't think there was any possibility the guy might still be alive, since the back of his head was missing.

Moving her flashlight around in the dark trunk to see what else might be stuffed in there, Kate only saw the man, who had been dressed in jeans and a thin cotton shirt. Not wanting to touch the body until her supervisor, or a detective arrived, she stood up and backed away.

What a way to end a shift, she thought.

The K9 unit pulled up and Jackson took his time getting out of the car. Kate wanted to light a fire under his ass. She'd lost the douchebag, but at least the K9 could catch him before he got to a main road and caught a ride. *Hurry the fuck up*, she thought as he casually opened the back door and put the leash on Sailor.

She really needed to stop swearing, but she'd been doing it since she was four, so it was sort of ingrained. Another wonderful trait passed on by dear old Mom. *Better than being a junkie*, she told herself.

"Do you know which way he went?" Jackson asked after Kate gave him the rundown on the situation.

"Not a clue. He was gone when I got here." It killed her to admit her failure.

"So much for getting off work before the next shift takes over," Williams said.

"Got someplace pressing you need to be?" Kate snapped.

"Yeah, my bed. It's been a long night."

"It's gonna get longer. Did you see what was in the trunk?"

Williams and Jackson followed her to the car. They both crouched down as she shined her flashlight into the opening of the trunk.

"Well, that blows," Williams said.

The sight of the dead body got Jackson's ass in gear. He took Sailor to the driver's side of the car for a good whiff, then set off on his trail.

Thank God the car accident hadn't woken too many people in the neighborhood. And those who did come outside to see what was going on quickly went back inside when they remembered how hot and humid it was.

"Crime scene tape, Williams," Kate said. "Let's get some up before the neighbors come nosing around."

Kate looked at her watch. Maybe she'd have a good excuse to miss the meeting after all.

The tow truck driver arrived at the same time as the fire department.

"Kate," the tow truck driver said.

Peculiar, Texas was a small town, so they used the same companies a lot. Kate had already seen Lou twice this week.

"Lou," Kate said. "We have cargo in the trunk, so we need to turn the car over and retrieve it before you load up the car."

"Cargo? Meth? weapons?"

"A body?" she said as if it were a question.

"Fuck."

"Yeah, that's what I said, too. Coroner is on his way, so as soon as we get the guy out, you can load the car."

"The guy?" Lou asked.

"What kind of body did you think I meant?"

"This keeps getting better and better." Lou walked back to his truck.

He talked to his partner, pointing to the car, then specifically at the trunk. The younger guy pulled the cable from the winch at the front of the truck and hooked it up to the frame of the overturned car, then stepped out of the way. Lou started the winch, pulling the car out of the ditch a little as it turned right side up.

We should be so lucky as to have the trunk pop right open, Kate thought as the trunk looked jammed on one side. Kate swore the trunk had been opened more when the car was belly up. But just the one side had somehow lifted, probably from the way the car crashed.

Kate offered, "We can pull out the back seat, and get to the trunk that way."

"This is easier than dragging a dead body through the car, and besides, we need to preserve the interior for evidence," the coroner said.

Kate startled at the sound of his voice, not having seen him arrive. She doubted there'd be enough evidence to help them, but who was she to say at this point? Then she went to the driver's side of the car and pulled a glove from her pocket. She slipped the glove on and doing her best not to touch anything, she leaned in through the broken window. "Pull now," she said as she pressed the trunk release button.

The trunk popped open. Kate walked back to join the officers. They stood gawking at the man with the back of his head missing. She silently patted herself on the back for being smart enough to try the trunk release.

Just like a lot of small towns, Peculiar had its share of drug problems, theft due to drug problems, and even a bit of prostitution, but murder rarely touched their town. Kate hadn't seen a dead body in the line of duty, not like this anyway. He had dark skin and a sleeve of tattoos on the arm she could see. The other arm tucked under him as he'd been folded and tucked into the trunk. His thin white cotton shirt had short sleeves and buttoned up the front. The fabric looked nicer than your average shirt, and she knew the jeans were expensive by the logo on the back pocket. Nothing you could buy around Peculiar.

"What the hell is going on here?" Detective David Peebles asked.

Kate wasn't going to let this asshole, who couldn't be bothered to get out of bed in a timely fashion, take control. He'd taken almost an hour to get there.

"You live ten minutes away." Kate looked at her watch. "It's been an hour since you were called."

"Darby, I don't need any lip from you. I was at the gym." He pulled on gloves. "Tell you what, since you were here first, you'll partner with me on this."

Kate shoved her hands in her pockets to keep herself from flipping him the bird. She wanted a CID position, so she needed to be civil. Mouthing off to a detective wasn't going to help her cause.

"Take it easy, Peebles, she's my officer, not yours," Sergeant Gwilly said.

Kate turned to see Zane Gwilly walking up behind her. He never failed to make her heart smile when she saw him, even when she was mad at him. Gwilly stood six foot something, had the build of an athlete, and kept his head shaved bald. She loved the look, and how it fit his facial features: large eyes, bushy brows, a wide nose, and thick lips.

"She's the one who caught this case, Sergeant, it's hers. I have a big case I'm working on, so she'll have to follow through, along with CID." Peebles pulled a wallet from the back pocket of the victim's jeans.

"I've got this, Zane," Kate said.

"Have you ever investigated a murder, Kate?" Zane asked.

"You're my sergeant; I think you know the answer." Between Peebles and Gwilly, Kate's anger came close to reaching a boiling point.

Peebles handed Kate the wallet. "He's all yours."

Kate opened the wallet. "Marco Lopez, age thirty-six." She went on to read the address on the license.

Johnson said, "It was his car." He held up the registration he pulled from the glove compartment. "Wow, so the driver shot and killed the owner of the car, stuffed him in the trunk, stole the car, then gets pulled over by a cop. What made you pull him over, Darby?"

"He rolled through a stop sign."

Johnson shook his head. "Moron."

Kate smirked at the irony. It only took a little over

an hour, a dead man, and a runner to finally get the registration. If only she hadn't lost sight of the car in the first place, they'd have the case wrapped up, and the driver in custody.

"We'll finish our investigation of the interior of the car back at the yard. I'll have it dusted for prints and see what else we can find." Peebles frowned. "Have you done the field inventory in the hour it took me to get here?" He looked pointedly at Kate.

"Nothing to inventory. The car is spotless," Johnson said.

"Your shift is over. Let Detective Peebles do his job," Zane said to Kate.

Peebles raised his hands. "This is hers, Gwilly, I'll be available for questions, but Kate's got this."

Zane looked like that Marine you didn't want to mess with. Kate knew first hand that he could be either a teddy bear or just a plain old bear, since he was also her ex-husband.

"I can stay. Sleep is overrated," Kate protested.

"Yesterday, you said you had an appointment with an attorney. I doubt that was cancelled between last night when you told me and now."

Kate groaned. "I don't even have time to go home to take a shower or change clothes."

"Glove up," Peebles said.

Kate showed her hands.

Peebles handed her plastic number cards. "Get on it then."

In a small town, there wasn't a specific crime scene

unit. If a cop caught the call, it was his crime, his job to get the details on paper, in photos, and catalog the evidence. Of course, there was always at least one other officer, usually a superior, who assisted at the scene.

Cards placed, photos taken, evidence gathered into evidence bags and logged, they all stood back for a breather. Kate felt a small thrill at the thought of solving her first homicide.

Zane stepped up next to Kate. "Go. We'll get everything under control here and you can come in early for your shift tonight."

"Aren't you going home?" she asked.

"I'll see you tonight. Good luck today," he said as he walked back to his car. He turned back to her. "You'll have a lot of paperwork, so be prepared."

Chapter 2

Driving to her appointment across town, she concentrated on the details to put in her report. She normally wouldn't leave her shift without writing a report, but Zane knew she'd get it done. Besides, she had the radio call and her chest camera to fill in any details she might have forgotten, though she wasn't looking forward to seeing the dead man again on the video.

Between the runner, the homicide, and her meeting, she would've been hot without the sun bearing down. And thinking about having had a family close by, who she never knew, made her curious. How can a family go more than thirty years without a peep, when they lived in the same town? The idea of it made her grip the steering wheel tighter.

Pulling into the parking lot of the law office, Kate parked and took a minute to breathe and calm herself. No need to get her panties in a ruffle for something she had no control over.

The adrenaline of the morning's events had worn off, and she could really use a cup of coffee. Iced coffee. The temps never got below eighty in the overnight hours, and now with the sun out, the air felt like an aquarium. She'd grown up with this weather and never minded it as a kid. As a grown up, she had to wear a t-shirt, Kevlar vest, and a uniform, along with a twenty-five-pound duty belt and long pants. Kids didn't care because they wore shorts and sleeveless shirts and ran through the sprinklers. What she wouldn't give to run through a sprinkler right now.

Reaching back to pull the hair tie from the bun at the nape of her neck, she reached up with her other hand to pull the visor down and look at herself. She shook her head to let her long brown hair fall in waves down her back, then touched the bags under her eyes. "Whatever." She flipped the visor back up, grabbed her purse from the back seat and got out of the car.

She hoped she didn't smell like she'd just worked a fourteen-hour shift, but she wasn't about to check on her way into the office. Having to wear her uniform to the meeting was bad enough.

The attorney's office, located on Griffith Street, had its own square block. It was a Gothic revival home positioned in the middle of the huge lot, surrounded on all sides by immaculately clipped lawns and severely trimmed boxwoods. She moved up the red brick walkway at a good clip. Now that she was here, she didn't want to be late.

Opening the white wooden door, she stepped into

the cool interior with its marble floors and dark wood walls that looked to be original to the house. A long mahogany desk graced the entrance about twenty feet from the door. A massive fan whirred overhead.

She walked up to the woman standing behind the desk. Dressed in a tight black pencil skirt and pale pink silk blouse, the woman made Kate self-conscious of her uniform. At least she'd had the wherewithal to leave her duty belt in her car.

"I'm here to see Mr. Norris," Kate said.

The woman smiled a trained smile. "Ms. Kate Darby?"

"Yes."

"He's on a call at the moment. Please have a seat and I'll let him know you're here." She held out her hand to indicate the seating area behind Kate.

Kate took a few steps in that direction, but decided to stand. She didn't want to be here long, and if she sat down, she'd pull out her phone and send Zane a text to check on the progress of the homicide case.

"Can I get you a cappuccino or water? We have a delicious white chocolate latte."

Kate's mouth almost watered at the thought. "The latte sounds delicious, thank you."

The woman picked up a headset from the desk and adjusted it over her head, then moved the mouthpiece. She pressed buttons on her console, then spoke quietly into the phone.

Kate looked around the room at the framed images of plantations, cotton for miles, and the workers who busted their asses in the hot sun to make sure the cotton business was profitable. Historically, cotton was primarily grown in East Texas, though now it had migrated south and west. Cotton had given way to hay fields and pecan groves. Or was it pecan orchards? She could never remember. This law office must have been in business for more than a century, or they just liked it to look as if it had history.

"Miss Darby, Mr. Norris will see you now."

Kate noticed the fabric of the receptionist's skirt as she escorted her to what Kate assumed would be Mr. Norris' office. She smiled when she realized her skirt was made of some sort of stretch fabric. She looked slick, but still comfortable. Smart woman. And she had a cushy job in an air-conditioned office. Smarter yet.

Opening the door to Mr. Norris' office, the woman stood in the hall as Kate walked past her and into the room.

"Thank you, Miss Eva," Mr. Norris said.

Eva shut the door.

A tall, fit looking man of about forty stepped out from behind the desk to greet her. He had a full head of gray hair, trimmed short on the sides, and a little too long on top. His tanned skin told her he liked outdoor sports. Tennis? Golf? Who cared? She just enjoyed looking at him and his blue eyes framed with well-established wrinkles.

"I'm Victor Norris. Sorry for the last-minute call regarding this matter." He shook her hand quickly and didn't give her another glance. She glanced at his backside as he turned around to walk back to his seat. "Please have a seat."

The office had the same décor as the entry, only the floors were a natural dark wood, and the walls were floor to ceiling bookcases. Kate sat in the leather chair and stared across the long desk with ornate carvings around the edges and down the legs.

"Sorry I didn't have a chance to change my clothes before coming. My shift ran overtime. Dead body and all." What the hell was she saying?

"Oh, I'm sorry." He didn't sound sorry; he sounded like he wanted to get on with it.

"But I'm here," Kate said, feeling like a kid in the principal's office.

Victor straightened the papers on this desk into three piles, then picked up a folder off the top of the middle pile. "Before I read the will, I should let you know, you'll be the only one here today. Other than distant relatives, you're the only living relative, and the only one mentioned in the will."

Kate leaned forward. "How is that possible? I didn't even know I had a grandfather until yesterday, or last night, when your assistant called."

"Everyone has a grandfather, whether we meet them or not," Victor said. "And I'm sorry you never met Edwin Barrow. You'd have liked him. I know I did."

Kate wondered if he said it because the old man was his client, not really meaning it. For some reason, she wanted Edwin to be an asshole. "I'm sure I wouldn't have. He had more than thirty years to reach out to me, and I only hear about him after his death."

"There are some things he asked me to explain before I read the will to you." Victor opened the file and flipped over the first piece of paper.

Kate stifled a yawn.

She heard a light knock on the door. Eva walked in and handed her a latte. Kate offered an awkward smile as she accepted the coffee. Not sure what she'd expected, but it certainly wasn't to be served her coffee in a to-go cup with a lid. From the décor of the interior of the building, she'd expected fine china, or at least a ceramic mug.

"Thank you, Miss Eva," she said.

Eva nodded, glanced quickly at Victor, then left the room.

Victor looked at Eva, then back at Kate. "Edwin spent a lot of time and money trying to find you. He didn't even know Amy had a daughter until after she died."

Kate didn't know why, but her heart hurt when she heard her mom was dead. She'd stopped checking up on her when she was in high school. Tried to pretend she was dead. The Darbys were her family, and when she let go of the hate and abandonment she gripped so tightly to, she realized the Darbys were not giving up on her.

"After she died?" That didn't even make sense.

"A nurse mentioned something about Amy talking to her baby during her delirium. Neither the nurse nor

Edwin knew if she was delusional, or if she really had a child. Edwin needed to know."

"When did Amy die?" For some reason, it bothered her that she didn't know.

"Ten years ago. Drug overdose," he said matter-of-factly with no empathy.

"Good to know," Kate said, not knowing what else to say. "Weird that it took Edwin ten years to find me."

"He had nothing to go on."

The sadness she felt made her angry, and she gripped the arms of the leather chair, feeling her fingers dig into the soft fabric. "I guess they weren't close."

"Edwin didn't have much contact with her in her adult years. They lost touch when she ran away from home as a teenager. He told me he'd enabled her enough, paying for motel rooms only to find out she use the room for prostitution. Giving her money for food only to realize what a fool he was. He said the last straw was when his assistant brought her several bags of groceries, and when he turned to walk away, Amy tossed the bags back out the door at him."

Kate chuckled. That was Amy all right. "She had her issues, didn't she?" The question was rhetorical.

"And Edwin washed his hands of her. Amy's mom left when she was only fifteen, and Edwin didn't have time to date back then. He had his pecan business, lived outside of town, and tried the best he could to give Amy the love and attention she needed."

"She needed a lot of attention. And the apple

didn't fall far from the tree. I was a terror as a child," Kate admitted.

"Edwin blames it on her getting her driver's license." Victor shook his head as he spoke. "Gave her a freedom he couldn't control. The first time he knew there was trouble, she didn't come home. The next morning, the local cops drove Amy's car to the ranch. Or as Edwin called it, the plantation. Amy was nowhere to be found."

Kate's heart hurt for a man she never even knew. She couldn't imagine how terrified he had to have been.

"There's a lot of history. The only reason Edwin knew Amy was dead was because she wore a locket. Just a cheap piece of base metal, and inside she kept his contact information. The nurses called him. Amy died before he got to the hospital. She was his only child, and it killed him that he couldn't save her."

She wanted to tell Victor about her mom. The life Edwin missed.

The apartment on Clark Street needed cleaning, but Kate didn't know any better. She sat cross-legged on the grimy kitchen floor, wearing worn pajamas, howling like a child who didn't get her way. Next to her, Amy Barrow, wearing cutoff denim shorts and a strappy tank top, lay on her back, her body rocking and convulsing, saliva foaming from her mouth, green vomit pouring down her right cheek had puddled on the floor, gradually making its way toward Kate's bare legs.

The clock read 7:14 (she'd be told the details many years later) when Kate heard the banging at the door. She looked at her mom, then looked at the door. She mustered the energy to stand and trudged to the door. "Help," she whispered, as she tried to reach the chain lock. After a few tries, she gave up, then twisted the door handle. "I can't get the door open."

The nice lady in the bathrobe and house slippers asked, "Is everything okay?"

Kate hiccupped with fear, unable to speak, tears rolling down her already soaked face. She shook her head.

The lady pushed her face against the restrained door to see inside. Kate looked back at the kitchen floor where her mother lay in a puddle of vomit and spit.

"Oh, shit," the lady said, then disappeared.

Any other time, Kate would have laughed and pointed. "She said shit. Shit, shit, shit." Her mother would have said, "Damn it, Kate, you can't say those words. You want me to wash your mouth out with soap?" She barely registered the word that morning.

Kate stood in the same spot near the door, shaking, watching the fabric on her pajamas move. The lady left her. She couldn't go back into the kitchen. Mommy scared her.

Kate heard sirens. She stood frozen in place, no longer shaking. Police were bad, her mom had said. She held her breath as the sirens got closer, she couldn't move from the spot by the door. Bad police were coming, and this was bad. The snot ran down her upper lip, into her mouth and she continued to cry.

The nice woman wasn't so nice. She called the police. Bad lady, *Kate thought.*

When the sirens stopped, she heard running. Someone coming up the stairs to the second floor. She was in trouble. Her mommy was in trouble. Bad police. She'd heard it so many times, and it was all she could think about.

She forced herself to go back into the kitchen. Grabbing her limp mom by the arm, Kate tried to drag her out of sight. Maybe to the corner near the stove. But her mom was too heavy. She plopped down onto the floor, breathing hard. "I'm sorry, Mommy."

Moments later, the door flew open with a bang as men, who were not the police, plowed into the apartment. Kate started crying again. Relief. It wasn't the police. Mommy would be okay.

The day the EMTs took her mom away was the last time she saw her. The selfish, drug addicted bitch never even tried to regain custody. And Kate knew she was alive, living in Sulpher Springs, because in her teens she got curious and looked her up. No death certificate, but an arrest record a mile long.

It had taken years for Kate to understand her mom wasn't coming back. Every night, she prayed to a God she didn't believe in, because just in case there was a God, her mommy might come back. She never saw anyone she knew back then again. Except the case worker; she saw her a lot.

Being a ward of the state sucked. Age had taught her that if there was a God, he answered her prayers, but in His way. Never seeing Amy again was a blessing that took her decades to understand.

"She didn't want to be saved," Kate said.

Victor pressed on, as if he needed to be somewhere. "Anyway, Edwin learned what he could from the nurse. He did his best to try and find you."

Kate rolled her eyes. "That was ten years ago. I wasn't hiding."

Victor picked up and turned another piece of paper. "Our private investigators found you within a year. But Edwin didn't want to disrupt your life. He saw how successful you are, and he said you looked happy."

What the hell did he know? Kate wasn't sure she'd ever really been happy a day in her life. Even as hard as Zane tried, nothing made her truly happy.

"Yeah, well, he got the successful part right. I'm a good cop."

Victor nodded. "So now you know. He didn't know about you in your lean times. Only after you'd become the brilliant young woman you are. And because of this, he left you his estate."

When she'd come in, she planned to jump out of the chair with indignation and refuse the old bastard's goodwill, no matter what it was. Now she decided to listen.

"If you have time today, I can take you by the plantation, but it will have to be after one o'clock. I have several other appointments."

"The plantation?"

"It's really just a farm located on the outskirts of Peculiar. It's been in his family for three generations. Originally a cotton plantation, now it's acres and acres of pecans. It obviously will skip your mother's generation, and it's now yours."

Kate still didn't understand. "He's leaving me a house?"

24

Victor nodded. "The entire property. There are many provisions in his will for the upkeep of the estate. He started leasing the pecan orchards to another farmer about five years ago, so you won't have to worry about planting and harvest seasons or any of that. And our office, along with his long-time accountant, will handle all of the financials."

She might like this. She'd been wanting to move to the country. "I now own a pecan farm?"

Victor smiled. "You do."

"I'm just a cop. I'm not sure I can afford the property taxes on this," Kate said, frowning.

"It's zoned for agriculture, so the property taxes aren't as high as you'd think. And again, there's a trust. It will cover all expenses relating to the home and land. Edwin's accountant has everything in order, so you won't be burdened."

Intending to go back to her apartment and take a nap, Kate barely sipped her latte, knowing the caffeine would keep her buzzed for a few hours at least. She took the cup with her as she left the lawyer's office, along with the thick folder, and a new appointment card.

It had taken an hour to go through the papers and sign documents.

According to Victor and the will, the house was hers, and all maintenance, housekeeping, landscaping, electricity, gas, insurances, and whatever else should come up, would be paid for by a trust managed by Edwin's financial advisors and the attorney's office. All

Kate had to do was live on the property, and sign papers saying she'd never sell the property or let it fall into disrepair. She also had to let the current renter of the pecan orchards have the first right of refusal for the lease when it was time to renew. And allow the renter to stay in the servants' home on the property rent free.

She wasn't sure she liked the part about the free-loader, but her grandfather probably had good reasons for allowing the person to stay.

Pulling into her parking space, she turned off her car, then picked up the paper with the address of her new house. She almost restarted her car to drive out to the farm, sure she'd driven by it at least a hundred times, not knowing it belonged to Edwin.

"Grandpa Edwin," she said, and it squeezed her heart.

After all the hate she'd felt since Eva's phone call, now she felt sadness and loss. That bitch of a mother had kept her from meeting her real family all these years. Made her think she was an orphan, not wanted or loved. "Fuck you, Amy," she said as she grabbed her coffee cup and the folder and got out of the car.

Between the runner, the dead body in the trunk, and learning she had a grandfather who loved her, sleep was not coming any time soon. She'd deferred the tour of her new home to the next day, so she could get back to the station to check the progress of her investi-gation. And it was definitely her investigation. One detective in the department didn't give him much time for more than a few murder cases. She'd investigate this because it was her traffic stop. If Zane tried to take her off it, she'd do the unthinkable and go over his head.

Sleep would not come, so she padded into the kitchen. Grounds, filter, water, brew. She could smell it brewing as she headed to the bathroom for a shower.

Chapter 3

Zane's patrol car spent entirely too much time in the parking lot of the station lately. He was a sergeant, and yet he'd been doing the work of a lieutenant for at least three months. He'd damn sure better get the promotion if he was going to be doing the work.

Zane had been sitting at his desk for more than an hour when Kate walked in without knocking. She sat down in the chair across from him.

"You look well rested," he said dryly, leaning back in his chair.

She stuck her tongue out at him. "What's the latest on our investigation?"

"*Our* investigation?" Zane said.

"Oh, come on, it was my traffic stop. I should get to investigate the homicide," Kate said.

"Stop whining. What happened at the attorney's office?" Zane changed the subject. He wasn't in the mood.

"I inherited a pecan farm off I-30, just east of town," she said, completely nonchalant.

Zane laughed. "That's a good one."

Kate leaned forward, her travel mug in her hand. "I'm serious. Apparently, I had a grandfather named Edwin Barrow, and he left me a pecan farm and an antebellum house."

The smile disappeared from Zane's face. He wasn't sure he liked this. She'd live further away, be more independent than she already was. At least he got to see her nearly every day, and for the most part, they worked well together.

"Congratulations, I guess." Zane leaned even further back in his seat. "That's going to be a lot of upkeep for one person to handle."

"You'd think." Kate blew on her fingernails and buffed them on the front of her shirt. "But, alas, the place comes with a staff and a trust. Grandpa Edwin wants to be sure the farm doesn't fall into disrepair. Everything has been taken care of. And if I need anything for the house, I just contact good old Victor. Actually, Eva, because I don't think Victor has time to take my calls. He barely had time to look at me this morning." Kate wiggled her brows. "But I got a good look at him."

Zane shook his head. It had only been six months since their divorce, and Kate made it clear every chance she got that she was on the prowl, so he'd be on the prowl, too. But he just couldn't make himself move on.

"Back to this investigation," Kate said.

"We'll be working it together. Do you think you can handle that? Peebles has a full plate with that domestic last week and another case he's working with the sheriff's department."

He hoped she wouldn't balk at working together. Maybe working this close was a bad idea. He'd let sleeping dogs lie, and he'd work this case without her if she didn't want to be a part of it. But he wasn't giving it to her to work alone or with anyone else.

"Cool. Get me up to speed," Kate said.

"First, you need to write up a report on your rookie. He's been riding with you for a week now."

Kate crossed her arms. "Oh, that. Fine, I'll write up my review. We work together again tonight. Then if the chief says it's all good, he'll partner with another officer for a few months, and I'll get my car back to myself."

"You had it to yourself last night," Zane said. "You like being alone, don't you?"

Kate put her hand out, like she was stopping traffic. "Don't even go there. Not up for discussion."

Zane sat forward in his chair and moved the pens around on his desk. "I didn't mean it like that. No need to be bitchy."

"Catch me up already. I want to get a move on with this case."

"I'll get you caught up, but we both need to get some sleep. Six o'clock is going to come fast, and as soon as the sun goes down, we'll both be exhausted."

"I'm good, just tell me already. Then I'll go back home."

Stubborn. Zane opened a file on his computer. "The car was wiped clean except for the driver's side."

"The jackass who ran?" Kate leaned forward, trying to look at his computer screen.

He moved it to a better angle. "According to the prints, your driver is Daniel Boyd."

Kate slapped the top of the desk. "That little snot. I thought I recognized him before he took off. Just didn't put him in a Mercedes. He's a 1985 Ford F150 kinda guy."

Zane laughed. Boyd was no stranger to Peculiar, Texas cops.

"We pulled the footage from your chest camera, which corroborates your story about him taking off. Sneaky little shit, stomping on the gas while he was still leaning over like he was getting the registration."

"I didn't see it coming until it was too late."

"Obviously," Zane said.

"And what about the dead guy?"

"We ran his name, and he's no saint either, just smarter. Every charge against him for the last three years has been dropped."

"What the hell?" Kate rested her elbows on Zane's desk.

"Most of the charges were drug related. Possession, possession with intent to distribute, stuff like that. All dismissed. I'm thinking he's a rat."

Zane had a pretty good idea of how the guy

worked. As long as a crime wasn't against another person, like assault, battery, burglary or theft, to name a few, a guy could offer up a bigger fish and get his charges lessened or dropped. If it was really good information, charges went away in the blink of an eye. This guy knew things. And if Zane was the betting type, he'd bet this guy had done a whole lot of talking.

"I wonder who he ratted out to end up in the trunk of his own car with his head blown apart?" Kate had a faraway look, as if she already had plans to investigate that angle.

"Good question," Zane said.

"And my runner?" Kate asked.

"Boyd's a small-time petty thief. Apparently, he's moved up to murder and grand theft auto." Zane tapped a few keys.

"We got an address on this weasel?"

"We do, and I sent a couple of uniforms to see if he's home. No answer."

"That's it? We need to find him."

"We've got a BOLO, and I got a warrant."

"We damn sure better. How often does the killer land in our laps like this?"

Zane stifled a laugh at her remark. She'd never investigated a homicide, so she had no idea how often a killer landed in their laps. Or maybe she did. She and Peebles being good friends and all. Then he really laughed.

"What's so funny?" She leaned back.

"Nothing. You been buddying up with Peebles, learning about murder investigations?"

Kate's face went blank, then she got it. "Screw you."

Zane laughed harder.

"Look, I've got a line on this. We've got eyes on the streets. Go home. Drink some hot tea, or whatever it is you do to relax. Be back here at four."

"Hot tea? Seriously? It's summer in Texas." Kate stood, shoving her travel mug in his face. "Even my coffee has ice in it."

"Whatever you need to do to relax, do it. I'm going home for a few hours. Neither of us is going to be worth a shit with no sleep. And if you don't go home, I'll make sure you don't work tonight. I don't need a sleep deprived officer behind the wheel of a patrol car."

"What other evidence did you find?" she asked, ignoring him.

"Marco Lopez was shot, then stuffed in the trunk of his own car. Boyd either took his car for one last joy ride, or he was moving the car to a different location, but never made it to his destination, thanks to you. We're still working on more evidence."

"The thing that bothers me is the car being wiped clean," Kate said.

"It may have been wiped completely clean if Boyd had made it to his destination. He didn't exactly have time to clean up his prints before he took off."

He saw the red rise from her neck, up across her

33

face. She'd lost her guy and bringing it up pissed her off.

She stood. "I'll be back in a few hours."

Zane stood and walked to his office door. He closed it behind her before she could argue or change her mind.

Once she was gone, he leaned against the door, closed his eyes, and sighed. He opened the door again and went back to his desk.

Everything about this case screamed drugs. Zane needed to connect Lopez to Boyd somehow. And he needed to see where it went. Who had Lopez snitched out to stay out of jail? He hadn't had time to look deep into Lopez, but he planned to do just that.

He sat down at his desk and fired up his computer again. "Who are you, Marco Lopez, and why don't I already know you if you're in my town?"

After twenty minutes of digging, Marco's history came to life. Even though his Mercedes was registered in Dallas County, he seemed to spend more time in East Texas than near Dallas. He had warrants in three counties. Minor crap: traffic violations, trespassing, failure to appear. Marco had to have some good intel in North Texas and East Texas, because he'd had charges dropped in Dallas, Clay, and Hunt counties.

Pulling up a booking photo, Marco didn't look like the kind of guy who drove a Mercedes. He looked rough around the edges, with hair that was too long, a patchy wannabe beard, and sad brown eyes.

"Who are you?" Zane asked out loud. "And what were you doing in Peculiar?"

Zane willed the image to talk, but Marco only stared back at him.

He looked up to see Chief Rambone standing in his doorway, about ready to knock. Zane waved him in.

"I hear it's been an eventful morning. Where's Darby?"

"You're in early," Zane said.

"Not really. I talked to Peebles. Wanna fill me in?" Rambone stepped into the room and leaned against the wall.

Zane thought it weird he didn't come in and sit down. Maybe he was busy and didn't want to get too comfortable. He gave him the lowdown on Darby's traffic stop.

"Shame she let the driver get away. This could have been all wrapped up." He looked past Zane, staring at the wall behind him.

"You know how it is. I'm just glad she didn't get shot or run over."

"Did the driver have a gun?" the chief asked.

"Who knows?" Zane said, thinking it was a stupid question. "He ran. We still haven't tracked him down, but we're working on it."

The chief pushed off the wall. "What about the house on M Street? Any more trouble?"

Swift change of subject.

"It's always something. I'm working on getting a

warrant to search the property. Hoping it comes in this afternoon."

"You've got probable cause?"

Zane didn't feel the need to explain all the work he and Darby had put into the case, so he said, "I do."

That seemed to be enough for Rambone. "Okay, well, keep me posted. I want to know when it goes down."

With that, Rambone left Zane's office. Zane felt exhaustion overwhelm him as he looked back at Marco's photo again.

Chapter 4

Even though he practically grew up in Peculiar, Jake Underwood felt weird being back and calling it home. He didn't even have his own place yet. He'd been too busy working since he finished at the police academy.

Jake's uncle, Tucker Simon, had run Lucien's Diner for as long as he could remember, and still did. Uncle Tucker opened his home to Jake until he could get settled. As far as Jake was concerned, Tucker had the coolest house on Caddo Lake. At least that's how he'd remembered it as a kid. Maybe not the biggest house, and maybe not the coolest *now*, but when Jake was a kid, it was heaven.

He stayed in Peculiar from Memorial Day weekend until the week before school started, and his uncle was so much fun. Little did he know back then, his mom was getting rid of them for the summer. To Jake and his little sister, Mom was sending them to summer camp.

Every day was a picnic: BBQ, boating, tubing, skiing. It was Jake's home away from home.

Now here he was, Officer Jake Underwood, working in the lake town of his childhood. He smiled at the thought.

Tucker walked into the kitchen while Jake was preparing a pot of coffee. "How's it going so far?"

He was already dressed in his Peculiar Police Department uniform, duty belt and all. "It's okay. I feel sorta stupid right now, but I'm learning."

Uncle Tucker looked just like Jake's mom. And Jake looked like her too, mostly. At fifteen, he'd already been taller than her, and at twenty-four, he stood six-one and tipped the scale at two hundred pounds. His mom stood barely five feet tall, a waif of a woman. His dad had been a jockey at tracks all over the south, only a little taller than his mom. Jake was glad he was built like Uncle Tucker, but without the belly. Yet.

"You have your own patrol car?" Tucker pulled the pot out of the machine before all the coffee had brewed.

"Uncle Tucker, now mine is going to be like brown water with no flavor."

He looked up at Jake through his bushy brows. "Who bought the damn coffee?"

Tucker had him there. Jake was a guest, eating his food, drinking his beer, and choking down his coffee.

"I have to ride with a seasoned officer for sixty days before I'm on my own." Jake poured the weak coffee into his cup and tried to drink it black. Or brown, as the case may be.

"Then what the hell did you go to the police academy for?" He twisted the wire tie off a loaf of bread and pulled two slices from the bag. As he popped them into the toaster he said, "I thought they taught you everything you needed to know."

He'd already explained it to him a dozen times, maybe more. "There's always more to learn."

Jake put the lid on his travel mug and headed out the door. "Maybe I can talk Kate into eating at Lucien's tonight. And shouldn't you be there already? I thought you were working nights this week, too."

Tucker grunted as a response. Jake knew Tucker had been trying to cut his hours back for years, but good management was hard to find, and even harder to keep. He expected Uncle Tucker would work eighty hours a week until the day he closed the doors on Lucien's Diner or died.

Living on the lake was different now. He didn't enjoy it as much. No time for boating or fishing. When he wasn't working patrol, he was studying or helping at the diner. Jake wanted to be the best cop he could be, and make his uncle proud that he'd come to work in Peculiar.

He sipped coffee as he left his uncle's house and got in his car. Turning on Lakeshore Drive, headed under the highway overpass to Flood Street, he looked at the clock on the dash. Even though he didn't expect any traffic he left early, wanting to be at the station before

Kate Darby arrived. She was his training officer, and she had been at the station every day that week before he was. Jake didn't want her to think he was a slacker, even though he'd never been later than fifteen minutes early.

He turned left on Flood Street and parked in the lot on Oak Street and low and behold, Kate's Expedition was already there. Damn, it was like she knew. He could see her texting when he walked up to the passenger side and tapped on the window.

She jumped like she'd been hit with a Taser, then flipped the switch to unlock the door. "Damn, you trying to kill me before the week is even over?"

Jake climbed in the passenger seat. If she wasn't his boss, Jake would have said Kate was gorgeous. Her long brown hair had blonde highlights, and when it wasn't pinned in a bun at the nape of her neck, it hung in curly waves. Everything about her screamed beauty, from her creamy skin to her curves. Even with that damned vest on, he could tell she was hot. But she was also tough as nails. At least that was the vibe he'd gotten so far.

She was a lot older than Jake, and her ex-husband was their sergeant. Gwilly never said anything, but the way he looked at her when she wasn't watching was the way every woman longs to be looked at. At least that's how he'd want to be looked at if he was a woman. Loved. Only Kate wasn't looking back. He wondered if she had moved on.

"I'm ready for my week to be over. You're a task master."

Kate laughed, and put her phone away. "You're too funny. Try riding with Gwilly for a few days, you'll be begging to have me back."

She was right. Much nicer to look at than old, bald Gwilly.

"What's on the agenda for today?" Jake leaned back in the seat.

"Caught a murder last night."

Jake sat up. "What? On my night off?"

"Sorry, dude, but you'll get to hang out with me and Gwilly while we investigate. Unless they move you to another car, which they might."

"I can't believe I missed out." Jake leaned back again, sulking.

"Not that you're glad a guy is dead or anything," Kate said.

"I'm not. It's just I always miss the good stuff." He settled into the seat.

"Don't get too comfy, we've got a meeting with Rambone before we get started." She unbuckled her seatbelt and got out of the car.

Jake followed.

Other than grilling him and taking him to task, Kate made work easy. She talked a lot and she kept him abreast of how things worked in Peculiar. Every department had rules in addition to what's taught at the academy, and some of them were best learned by doing.

Kate told him all about her runner and the guy in the trunk on the way to see the chief. She turned around and tossed him the keys. "You're driving tonight, Rookie."

He caught the keys but just barely, as she tossed them a bit short. Jake grinned wide. He'd been waiting all week to drive, and she kept putting him off.

Several officers had recently moved on to larger cities and Jake felt like Chief Rambone was happy to have new blood. Then, when he interviewed with the assistant chief, Esmeralda Oliverez, she didn't seem nearly as happy. He wondered if it was because he was white and male. Hiring him wasn't part of their Equal Opportunity Employer quota. He didn't see many other people applying for the job. Being a cop used to be a noble profession. The media had done their damnedest to change that perception.

"Been a quiet week so far, other than last night, which you missed. But this is Thursday night. Even with summer, the college kids get a little rowdy."

"Stop rubbing it in. It sounds like a long shift for you, though."

"It was."

Six at night to six in the morning, he had to admit, he liked a lot more than days. Kate explained it was because administrative personnel got off work at five, and there was less bullshit. Also, no old ladies calling dispatch to complain that the mailman didn't shut the door on their mailbox, or old men complaining about the neighbor mowing at seven in the morning and disturbing their morning coffee. The old men were the worst. No, old women were. Heck, it was a toss-up.

"I thought the chief was administrative. You know, working nine to five." Jake had yet to see him when he clocked in at six.

"The chief works when he needs to, be it nine to five, or nine to nine. Whatever. So be prepared and make it quick. I've been here for a few hours working on the case from this morning. I'm ready to get in the car and catch some bad guys."

They walked into Chief Rambone's office together, both sitting at the same time.

"Officer Underwood, you ready?" Chief Rambone said.

He thought the meeting a formality, but the look on the chief's face, and his tone made him think otherwise.

"I guess so, yes," Jake said.

"You know, that was a pretty shitty thing to do."

Kate and Jake walked back out to her vehicle to start the shift.

She just smiled.

"Suddenly at a loss for words?" Jake teased. "That's a first."

"I couldn't exactly tell you it was something good. That wouldn't have been any fun." She walked around to the passenger seat. "This is going to feel weird."

"Thanks anyway, and I appreciate you letting me drive." Jake unlocked the car and opened his door.

"Don't go all mushy on me now. We're going to have a long night ahead, and I'm not good at mushy."

"Yeah, I noticed." Jake said.

After the meeting with Rambone and his review after his week with Kate, the captain had given them goals for the evening.

It was only Thursday, but the way the schedule worked, it was Jake's last day of the week. He hadn't been on patrol the night before because of administration stuff he needed to take care of, but he was back and ready to roll. After tonight, he had three days off. Oddly, he wasn't looking forward to it.

As Jake drove out of the parking lot and headed back toward the lake, the town seemed different, somehow magnified, and smaller at the same time. Driving, answering the radio, and making the decisions, it was his baby. With Kate's approval, of course.

"Moved into your apartment yet?" she asked.

"Oh sure, in my spare time." Jake looked at her for a moment. "I'm moving in next weekend. I think my uncle will be happy to have the house back to himself."

"I'll bet he loves having you there. We'll have to stop by the diner for dinner tonight. I'll bet he beams with pride at seeing you in uniform." Kate looked out the passenger window, scanning the streets.

"Not sure he wanted this for me. And my mom's definitely not happy. But I've always wanted to be a cop."

"It's not a safe, nine to five, white collar job, that's

for sure. But I can't imagine doing anything else." Kate seemed to be on edge.

"Is it my driving?" Jake asked.

"What?"

"You're edgy."

Kate raised her hands and shook them out. "I am. I want this Daniel Boyd guy so bad my mouth is watering. They went by his house earlier today, but no answer. We're waiting for a search warrant to enter whether he answers or not."

Before they left his office, Kate discussed the events of the morning with the chief, and Jake sat silent, soaking in every detail, pissed he hadn't been working.

"I want to be there."

"For what?" Kate asked.

"The takedown. I want to be there when you find him and slap the cuffs on."

"We'll see."

They hadn't been on the streets an hour when they got their first call. Alcohol, hot sun, and the lake tended to bring out the worst in people. The dispatcher radioed in a domestic dispute.

Jake grabbed the mic. "229 responding."

"Use your own badge number, not mine."

Several other cars responded, too. They'd been taught at the academy that domestic disputes were some of the most dangerous calls. The situations were volatile, tempers flared, alcohol could be involved, and extreme caution recommended. Several deaths of brothers in arms had been on domestic calls. It had been a rough year for Peculiar's boys in blue, losing one of their own to an enraged ex-husband.

"To protect and to serve, whether you want it or not." Kate said, as they went Code 3 with lights and siren.

Jake had to admit, it was a rush to be behind the wheel and have the sea of cars split and let him through. Not a single asshole blocked their way as he sped to their destination on the other side of the lake. More often than not, he had noticed cars didn't always pull over for law enforcement. Several times while sitting in the passenger seat all week, he felt the urge to move his foot over, slam it down on Kate's and ram the idiots when they didn't get out of the way. Only somehow, he didn't think they were all idiots. Some were just defiant dickwads.

"Okay, Jake, we've talked about this. I lead the way. There will be several cars and probably an ambulance at the scene. Even the paramedics will be in danger if this is a nasty one. Be alert and be cool."

When they pulled up, three other vehicles had already arrived. He saw a sheriff's deputy and another Peculiar patrol, along with an ambulance. Kate and Jake parked behind the other cars, then walked to the scene.

Sergeant Gwilly happened to be the Peculiar cop. As they approached, he said, "Officer Underwood. Darby."

A deputy spoke to a woman on the porch. In front of him, a man of about sixty, wearing a royal blue

Speedo, sat on the lawn, his hands cuffed behind his back. He had his legs spread, leaving plenty of room for his belly to sag between them. Jake heard the deputy explaining, "No matter if you want to press charges or not, someone's going to jail. We just need to get both sides of the story."

Gwilly pointed to the man in cuffs. "I want you and Underwood to talk to this guy. I'm going to take the woman and put her in the back of my car. There's another deputy on the other side of the house, talking to the guests at this little gathering."

"What's the deal?" Kate asked.

"Apparently these two have had too much to drink, and someone landed in the fire." He pointed to the bonfire next to the lake.

"Alcohol involved. Hard to believe." Kate rolled her eyes.

"Let Underwood ask the questions. I want you only to observe."

Jake walked to the man sitting on the lawn, trying to look like he'd done this a hundred times. "Hello, sir. Would you mind telling me what happened here tonight?"

The man looked up at Jake and promptly projectile vomited, liquid running down his chin onto his hairy chest and belly. He then rolled over on his side and passed out.

"That went well," Jake said.

Kate giggled and said, "You have quite a unique method of getting your guy to talk."

He wanted to puke. Vomit and other bodily fluids tended to make his stomach turn. "Shit."

"Nope, that's puke." Kate laughed aloud.

Everyone turned to look at them. Then Gwilly strolled over to see what was so damned funny. "What's the deal?"

"I don't think we'll be getting the story from him." Jake nudged him with his boot.

"No need. The witnesses by the fire said the woman was the aggressor. We can take the cuffs off this guy. I'm taking the woman back to the station to book her on domestic battery." Gwilly leaned down and took the cuffs off. The man twitched, but didn't wake up.

"You sure he's okay?" Jake asked.

From his back side, Kate leaned down and checked his pulse, then put the beer can he'd been drinking from in front of this nose and mouth. Jake could see the condensation as the man breathed in and out.

"He's fine." She looked behind her. "One of you people want to come and keep an eye on your friend here?"

"I got it," a young girl dressed in a barely there bikini said.

To the EMT, Kate said, "Wanna take a look at this guy? Make sure he's not going to die."

The EMT, who looked to be about Jake's age, jogged up to them.

They all looked at each other, then a younger guy of about twenty stepped forward and said, "Are you taking my mom to jail?"

Gwilly asked, "Is that your mom in the back of my car?" He pointed to his vehicle.

The kid nodded.

"You want to talk to her before we take her in?"

He shook his head and looked at the ground.

Jake and Kate trailed after Gwilly as he walked to his car. Kate asked, "Any more complaints on that house on M Street?"

"Oh, yeah, I was going to tell you, I wrote up the affidavit." He looked back at his detainee. "Why don't you let the kid drive your car back, and you can ride with me? Easier than transferring her to your car. I hate transporting women."

There was protocol for transporting the opposite sex. They had to call in to dispatch with the location, log what time they left the scene, then call in again to log in arrival time. The number of minutes to get from location to location would be determined, to make sure no one made a stop on the side to do the nasty, or any other illegal stuff.

He'd have killed to be a fly on the dashboard of that car as they drove back to the station. The M Street house had been the bane of their existence throughout the week. Calls about the traffic, the people coming and going at all hours, and general complaints that they thought it was a crack house. Jake and the other cops knew it was a crack house, but they needed proof to make any arrests.

Jake hoped they had a warrant and were going to bust the joint, but he wasn't privy to that conversation, though he did hear Kate and Zane discussing a warrant as they walked away.

There were no other issues at this call, so he got back in his car to follow his bosses back to the station.

Jake wasn't sure why he was so eager for a big bust, knowing there'd be plenty to come in the future, but he would say later, he never expected what happened that night.

Chapter 5

Before they even started the shift that night, Gwilly had filled out the affidavit for the warrant on the house on M Street. By the time they did the paperwork and got the domestic assault woman into the holding cell, Gwilly had the warrant.

The plan was to go to the house after dark, so the neighbors wouldn't see them coming, and warn the occupants of the house. If the neighbors were buyers, they wouldn't want their well to dry up. As Kate said, it would suck to have them flush all of the evidence down the toilet and have nothing for their efforts. It had happened before, and it would happen again.

After a few more hours on the street and a dinner break, they assembled at the office and Gwilly laid out the strategy for taking down the house. The butterflies in Jake's stomach had him wishing he hadn't eaten the second helping of Dutch apple pie at his uncle's place.

When they jumped in the car, Kate still let him

drive. He worked to streamline his focus. They were going into yet another dangerous situation, and he'd only been a real cop for a week. If the night went well, he'd have three days off to mentally pat himself (and the others) on the back. If not, Jake had three days to reassess if this was really the right career. In his mind, it went down smooth, but he knew it could all go sideways in a heartbeat.

"Things are going to happen fast. This is a no-knock warrant. We'll be breaching the door, and all hell will likely break loose. Be alert," Zane said before sending everyone to their vehicles.

The plan in place, and him being the rookie, he held the battering ram. A no-knock warrant meant they weren't required to announce themselves.

Parked halfway up the block, Gwilly gathered everyone around the hood of his car. "Bugger, you and Hanson are going to take the back. Underwood will go through the front with us. He's big and can work the battering ram."

"Do we have cars at the ends of the block?" Kate asked.

"We do. All escape routes have been secured as much as possible. There will be some runners, but we have a good idea as to the number of people in the house. Bugger has been watching since early today. He's working overtime for us on this one."

"Everyone, get to your places and radio in quietly."

Bugger and Hanson jogged up the block and disappeared into the shadows behind the house. Luckily, this neighborhood didn't have many fences and the house in question had only one short cyclone fence that even a five-year-old could leap in a single bound.

"We are going in fast before we cause a scene. On my count…go."

Dressed in full riot gear with helmets and shields, they ran to the front porch of the house. As they ran, Jake noticed people coming out of the house two doors down. "Shit."

"Cops, cops!"

Kate yelled, "Run!"

"Go, go, go," Gwilly yelled. "Get the damn door open."

Jake kicked into another gear he didn't know he had, took the porch steps in one leap and slammed the battering ram into the front door. It splintered like balsa wood. He barely stepped a foot to the side when Kate and Zane burst through the door.

The yelling and screaming hurt Jake's ears. Or maybe it was the chaos of half a dozen people running in different directions. He saw three people run up the stairs to the second floor, and a few more run to the back of the house. He tried to take it all in, to know who was where, in case he needed to assist or pull his weapon.

He wasn't sure where the bathroom was, but he bet more than one person ran that direction. No one bothered with the guys headed out the back door; they wouldn't get far. Their concern was with the interior of the home. Secure the evidence and make sure it didn't get flushed or washed down a drain and detain the occupants. That was their job.

"I'm going upstairs," Kate said as she flew by him. "Get the kitchen. Hanson and Bugger won't be able to stop all of them."

Jake ran into the kitchen where he grabbed a skinny white dude in dirty boxer shorts by the hair of his mullet. He yanked him back from the kitchen sink where the guy was opening Ziploc baggies, washing the contents, which looked like weed, down the drain. He hadn't even gotten a good head start before Jake shut him down. He fought like a mad dog, flailing his arms and kicking out with his legs. The front flap of his boxers parted and now his pecker joined his arms in the flailing.

"That's enough, dirt bag," Jake said, catching him with his own leg and taking him to the floor.

A moment of shock came over Jake as he realized the moves he'd learned at the academy worked. Dirt Bag lay flat on the floor, squirming like a ladybug on its back. Jake had to make himself breathe through his mouth (the guy stunk like rotten meat) as he rolled the guy over and put a knee in his back, fighting to get his arms in a position to get the cuffs on. "Give me your arm, asshole."

Geez, this guy could fight, still kicking as if it would help him. Jake thought he heard a muffled "Screw you."

Fighting for his own breath, Jake said, "Stop fighting, you're not gonna win this one." He struggled to get

Dirt Bag's arms behind his back. At least he knew the guy didn't have a weapon on him, unless his boxers had a secret compartment. What he wouldn't have given for some assistance, he thought, as he finally got the guy in cuffs. He remained with his knee on Dirt Bag's back while he took a few deep breaths and prepared to stand. He waited an extra minute before he finally stood, thinking he should have wrestled in high school, not played baseball.

Jake lifted him from the ground to stand him up, but Dirt Bag went limp. Why make it easy? "Either put your feet on the ground, or I'll do it for you. I guarantee you won't like my method."

"Fuck you. Police brutality, man. You have no right to be here. I know my rights." Breathing hard between words, he wanted to have his say.

"Put your fucking feet on the ground, or I will drag your ass out of this house by your hair." He wouldn't, but it sounded good.

"Do it, asshole, I don't give a fuck." He dropped like dead weight.

Jake let the scrawny guy fall to the floor. Where the hell was he going to go in boxers and handcuffs?

Looking up, he saw Gwilly had two men in cuffs on the living room floor and his hand on his shoulder radio, calling for more officers. "We'll need three more cars for transport."

Jake marveled at how quickly it all went down. Gwilly's team worked well together. He really wanted to be a part of this kind of family. It wasn't his bust, but he did get the door opened and cuffed the guy in the kitchen, so now he stood with his guy and waited for directions. As a rookie, he wanted to be an asset, not a liability.

Looking through the doorway, Jake saw Kate bringing a woman down the stairs. The chick wore floral stretch pants with a navy, green, and white color palette, and a spaghetti strap tee that was probably white at one time. He looked to her bare feet and noticed her painted toenails. He found it strange that she looked like she hadn't washed or cleaned her clothes in weeks, yet her toenails were painted perfectly in a bright pink.

When he looked up, he saw the grimace on her face. Did he also see a flicker of recognition? There was no doubt, they recognized one another immediately. Jake continued to stare at her, but she immediately dropped her gaze to the ground.

"Kim?" Jake couldn't believe it was the same Kim Vega he'd known as a kid.

She nodded almost imperceptibly, but didn't look up.

As Kate walked by, she said, "Friends?" Then she said something he didn't understand. Something about her name being Betty?

Jake shrugged, letting them pass without saying another word.

Kim's blonde hair hung down to her shoulders like spaghetti stuck to a wall. It looked like it hadn't been washed in days or trimmed professionally in years.

Ragged ends that had likely broken off from lack of nutrition. From the looks of her dark roots, she'd been lightening it somehow. No way she was going to a salon. She didn't look like she'd waste good drug money on professional hair color.

Kim's parents had a small cabin on Caddo Lake. They'd met there as kids. It was only two houses down from Uncle Tucker's place. Kim and Jake laughed away the summers, riding the inner tube behind his uncle's boat or early morning fishing. They shared secrets, dreams, and even suntan lotion. He had a huge crush on her, and went into depression every August when his parents came to get him. He hated going back home.

One summer, Jake remembered, he begged them to let him live with his uncle year-round so he could go to school in Peculiar. His parents refused, not wanting to hear another word about it. That was his last summer at the lake. Once he started high school, his schedule was too busy to spend the summers in Peculiar.

Every fall, the crush he had on Kim faded in the months after school started, then started again the first time he saw her in June. He never had the nerve to tell her how he felt. How he'd longed to touch her sun-bleached hair, hold her hand, and maybe even steal a kiss. He was too young and shy to do or say anything. Maybe that was for the best.

Over the years, he thought about her periodically, especially when they visited Uncle Tucker. But her parents sold the cabin, and Jake never saw her again. A few times, he tried looking her up on Facebook, but her name didn't come up. He'd catch himself wondering what had happened to her, who she'd married (if she had married at all), or if she stayed in Peculiar. He never guessed she'd be a junkie, or that he'd be arresting her in a drug raid.

Jake wanted her to look at him. Wanted to see if there was any hope left in her blue eyes, or if all hope had faded years ago. But she refused to look in his direction.

A cop came in from the backyard, picking Dirt Bag up off the floor, and dragging him outside. As Jake bent over to pick up the battering ram, the yelling started again. He flipped the snap on his holster and put his right hand on his gun. When he got to the top of the stairs, he saw Officer Dornan in a tug of war with a tall, skinny guy wearing a grey wife beater tee and baggy jeans. In the wrestling, the guy's jeans slid down his legs, revealing his lack of underwear. Jake glimpsed the guy's privates a few times as he flipped over during the confrontation. He'd seen enough shriveled penises for one night. He dropped the battering ram, moving his hand from his gun to his Taser.

Dornan wasn't able to get to his Taser, as he was trying to keep Numb Nuts from getting his gun. Jake aimed and tagged Numb Nuts dead center between his shoulder blades. For one, maybe two, seconds, he froze. It was enough time for Dornan to free himself, but then Numb Nuts blew through the jolt of electricity like a man possessed.

What the hell kind of drugs was this guy on? Numb Nuts

wasn't about to let fifty thousand volts of electricity ruin his high. Jake sent another jolt that dropped him to the floor. Dornan pounced, and had Numb Nuts' hands behind his back and the cuffs wrapped around his wrists before Jake could blink. Damn, his technique was good, once he had the guy in the right position. He'd have to ask him about that. Numb Nuts didn't even realize he'd been cuffed until it was too late to fight it.

Jake stepped forward and grabbed the guy by one arm, as Dornan grabbed the other, and they lifted him off the floor. Jake saw him look up with disdain, then roll his eyes and go limp. He wasn't going to make it easy on them. Jake maneuvered to keep from moving the prongs in the guy's back as they assisted him toward the stairs.

Numb Nuts would be assessed by EMS before they took him to the jail.

"Go ahead, douche bag, I'm adding resisting arrest to your list of charges."

As if he wasn't adding it already.

Numb Nuts decided to come to just long enough to look up and spit at Dornan. Yeah, that went over well. Dornan dropped his side of the guy and pulled a handkerchief from his front pocket. "Add assault on a police officer." Dornan wiped the spit off, then tied the handkerchief around the guy's face. "Oh, wait, you already have the assault charge. I'll add more."

Jake noticed some saliva had landed on Dornan's chest camera and looked down to be sure he had turned his on. He had. Kate had made sure it was so routine he didn't even remember turning it on. It's just what he did every time he exited the car, like locking the door. Kate had trained him well on this point.

What she hadn't talked to him about was what happens when you know the subject you're arresting and at one time in your life, you thought you were going to marry her.

Chapter 6

Kate watched the front door split open like balsa wood, as if it were hollow. Who knew, maybe they had used an interior door for the exterior. It sure seemed that way, but Kate didn't have time to slow down and inspect it. Jake hit the door hard once, and they were in.

People scattered like cockroaches when the lights turned on, only these cockroaches had no place to hide. The officers had their orders, and while Zane and Jake handled the first floor, she and Dornan ran up the stairs to catch whoever was on the second floor. At the top of the stairs, a skinny chick slammed directly into her. Thank goodness the girl was a waif, or the impact would have knocked Kate off her feet. As it was, she had to grab the railing to keep from falling back onto Dornan.

"You okay?" he asked.

"Fine. I've got her, you check the other rooms," Kate said, her voice a little unsteady.

She hated that she sounded scared. She wasn't. This was the type of night she lived for. Sometimes she thought about applying to the U.S. Marshals, so she could track fugitives and knock down doors on a regular basis. Alas, she couldn't leave Peculiar, as much as she wanted to; the place held her like an industrial magnet. She tried to leave three times in her life. The longest she stayed gone was three months.

Kate repositioned herself and had cuffs on before Raggedy Ann knew it. Kate shoved her up against the wall. "If you move, I'll shoot you."

"Fuck you," she said.

Kate pulled her Taser. "Fine, I'll give you a good zap instead."

That shut her up. That scenario had real possibilities of actually happening, and the girl knew it.

While watching her detainee, Kate kept an eye on Dornan, who'd done a good job of entering the rooms safely. These druggies came armed and dangerous when they were dealers. It wasn't unheard of for a guy to come out of a closet, guns blazing.

Dornan came back out into the hallway. "I've got one who might need medical assistance. He's out cold, but still breathing."

"Radio for medical and keep an eye on him. I'm taking this one downstairs."

Kate pulled the girl away from the wall, standing

behind her as she escorted her to the stairs. She finally had a chance to look around, and she looked down to see the girl wore no shoes, then she looked at the carpet. She was pretty sure a kid could grow science experiments in the stains. No way would she walk bare-footed in this house, she thought as she walked by a syringe with a bent needle stuck in the loop of the brown Berber.

Slowly making their way down the stairs, Kate looked at the greasy stringy hair matted at the back of the murmuring girl's neck. She concentrated on the words, barely making them out.

"Cunt. Motherfucking cunt. Stupid, stinking..." she kept repeating it on a loop.

As they came down the stairs, Kate saw Jake standing in the doorway of the kitchen. The look on his face reflected confusion. What could he be confused about? Then he opened his mouth. He knew the girl. Or at least he thought he did, apparently, and called her Kim.

"Friends?" she asked as she walked by, then added, "She's one angry Betty."

Jake moved to the interior of the house as Kate walked out the kitchen door.

"You're hurting me," Kim's words clear as can be.

"You'll be fine, Kim," Kate said. "Maybe I can get your boyfriend to come check on you in a few minutes."

"You probably got him in cuffs, too," she mumbled.

"I was talking about Jake." Kate opened the back door of her Expedition and helped Kim inside.

Fully expecting Kim to start kicking or banging her head, Kate stood outside the door for a moment before heading over to Zane and the others.

The murmuring died to almost nothing as Kate joined them. This made her suspicious. It wasn't like the other officers to stop talking just because she walked in the room. She could swear more creatively than they could, and vulgar stories didn't bother her. They knew that. But the silence was followed by stares.

"What, do I have a bugger hanging out of my nose?" She rubbed the back of her hand across her nose, just in case.

Johnson was the first to step back from the group, revealing a man standing with his hands on his head.

"Fuck me," Kate said aloud. "Danny Boyd."

"This will save us some time. But I'm still using that warrant to go through his house," Zane said.

"Who caught him?" she asked.

"Hiding in the bushes on the side of the house," Deputy Hensley said as he continued to pat him down.

"Just like a snake," Kate said. "That raid was a kill two birds kinda job."

Hensley nodded. "I heard about the car accident this morning. Guy with half a head."

"It was more than half," Zane said. "But not by much."

"Any leads?"

Kate pointed to Boyd. "He's our one and only suspect. Does it get any easier?"

Kate saw something small and white drop to the ground next to Boyd's foot. She walked over to get a better look.

"Leave it," Hensley said.

"I've got gloves on still," Kate said and picked up the tiny white plastic wrap, tossing it onto the hood of the deputy's car.

"There's more where that came from," Hensley said. "Spread your feet."

Boyd didn't move.

"I said, spread your feet. And I mean wide."

When Boyd still didn't comply, Hensley used his own foot to assist, kicking between Boyd's feet until he moved them apart. Bringing Boyd's hands down from his head, he cuffed him.

"You want me to shake him, or hold him while you do?" Zane asked.

"I can do both."

Hensley proceeded to hold Boyd by the cuffs with one hand and grab his butt cheeks with the other and shake. Then he grabbed him by the too large cutoff jean shorts and gave him a wedgie, then pulled the shorts back down. Along with the shorts came four more baggies of meth.

"Dude, were you going to sell those straight out of your asshole? That's disgusting," Kate said.

"That ain't mine. Don't know where that shit came

from." He looked over his shoulder. "You put that there to frame me!"

Hensley laughed. "Yeah, I've never heard that one before."

"If you got more up there, you'd better shake it out. The jail isn't as nice about it as we are. You'll just rack up more felony charges."

Zane grabbed him by the elbow. "I'll transport him, if it's all the same to you."

"Did you read him his rights?" Kate asked.

Hensley nodded.

"Daniel Boyd, you're under arrest for the murder of Marco Lopez…" Just to make sure, Zane read him his rights again.

Kate only heard the murder because Zane started walking away, but knew he had a laundry list on him at this point.

Kate didn't think the man could get any paler under the mercury vapor lights, but he did.

"What the fuck? What you talkin' 'bout? I ain't never killed nobody!" He wrenched his arm away from Zane.

Kate jogged to catch up.

"Does this mean you want to talk to us?" Zane said.

"Talk to you about what? Somebody dead and you pinnin' it on me because you can't make any other charges stick?"

The Peculiar cops and the county had made plenty of charges stick when it came to Boyd. He even had an active warrant. Not the one for murder, but another one for failure to appear.

"Want me to read you the charges that have stuck over the years? Hell, I even remember arresting you as a juvenile," Zane said.

Kate turned away with a smile on her face. They had this guy dead to rights. Then she turned back. "I already have you for fleeing, Danny boy."

"Don't call me that. I fucking hate that."

"What? Danny boy?" she said it again just to irritate him.

"I wanna talk to my lawyer," Boyd said.

Zane shot Kate an exasperated look. "See what you did? Now he's not going to tell us about the guy in the trunk."

Boyd tried to spin around and look at Zane. "What guy in the trunk?"

"Nope, never mind, you need to have your lawyer present," Kate said.

"That's bullshit, I can answer whatever I want. Then I can stop answering if I want my lawyer." He'd been read his rights enough, he could probably recite his Miranda rights word for word.

"You've already asked for a lawyer, Danny. You can't take it back now. Besides, I never thought I'd say this, but it might be best you have someone present." Zane steered Boyd to his car.

Hensley shook his head. "The guy you found in the trunk, you think Boyd killed him?"

Kate shrugged. "His prints are the only ones in the car."

"Seems a little too convenient," Hensley said and walked back to his vehicle.

Kate stared after him. "You wish."

But as she turned to watch Dornan and Underwood dragging an almost lifeless body out of the house, she chewed on what Hensley said.

"This is the last one," Dornan said.

"I see he's being cooperative," Kate said.

"He's pretending he passed out or something, but he doesn't know what real dead weight feels like. Besides, his scrawny ass doesn't weigh much. Fighting him would have been harder. Bet he has some sore arms from being dragged from the house."

The guy stirred, getting his foot underneath himself, then standing. Guess he hurt too much to pretend to be out of it any longer. And hearing it wasn't such a hardship for the cops made it less appealing.

"Put him in Dornan's car. Mine already has a passenger," Kate said.

Underwood looked at Kate, then back to her car. Kate thought she saw a smile turn up the corners of his mouth.

"You want help getting this guy into your car?" Underwood said.

"I'm good. I can fold him in half easily if need be." Dornan shoved the guy toward his car.

"Let's roll," Kate said. "I don't want that Angry

Betty in my car any longer than need be. She'll probably do something you'll have to clean up."

"Me?" Underwood asked.

"You're the rookie, not me." Kate walked around to the driver's side, then looked across the hood at Underwood.

He tossed her the keys. "Her name is Kim, not Betty."

Kate didn't bother to tell him, she knew her name wasn't Betty, it was just an expression.

Chapter 7

Kim sat in the back of Kate's cruiser, rocking back and forth, her hair a mask in front of her face. Jake sat in the passenger seat, wanting to reach back and move the hair for her, but the cage was in the way. It wasn't a good idea, anyway.

Kate called in the transport and drove back to the station. She kept looking at Jake with just her eyes, not even slightly turning her head, as if he wouldn't notice. Jake turned slightly sideways in the seat, watching Kim.

"You act like we've never had a person in the cage," Kate said with a hint of annoyance.

"It's not that." Jake adjusted in the seat to face straight forward, trying to concentrate on anything but Kim. But his brain kept going back.

She was twelve or thirteen the last time he saw her. Tall and skinny, with long straight hair and huge blue eyes. So much hope. Jake remembered she wanted to be a doctor, a nurse, or a dental hygienist. He laughed at her indecision, because he always knew he wanted to be a cop. He just happened to do it by way of the Army.

Everyone told him to get an education first, so he could go into the military as an officer. But if he knew what he wanted to do with his life, why get an education he didn't need? The military was an excellent education on what he didn't want for his life. He loved his guys, and loved the travel, but he didn't love the sandbox. He wanted to be a hero to someone, even if it was for rescuing their cat from a tree. In the sandbox, everyone hated them, even though they needed them. He expected that was why they hated the Americans, because they didn't want to need them.

He looked back at Kim, and wondered who would get her cat out of the tree, and how it got there in the first place.

Kate socked him hard on the shoulder. "That's enough! We'll be having a talk after we get her booked."

Jake rubbed his shoulder. "Ouch."

"Well, start acting like a man, and not a lovesick boy, and you won't get punched."

He could feel anger radiating off Kate. Nothing he could do. She'd be mad if she wanted to be. He'd do his best to be a good cop. Do his job.

The booking process didn't take long. Kate and Jake escorted Kim to a holding cell, then Kate took over. She insisted he find something else to do.

The something else he found was running Kim's

arrest record. It was only a matter of seconds before he slumped in the chair.

"Buddy, you should be on cloud nine, not sitting there like you just lost your dog." Gwilly slapped Jake on the back.

Jake straightened. "It was exciting. Thrilling even. Maybe I'm coming down off the high."

In truth, once he saw Kim, the high had worn off pretty quickly. Even taking down Numb Nuts, he had Kim's welfare in his head. Was Numb Nuts her boyfriend? Husband? The person who got her into this mess?

"It happens. Like a drug, only in a good way. If you loved this, you're in the right career."

Zane Gwilly had been in the military, too. He'd done his tours in Iraq, or was it Afghanistan? Jake could never remember and wasn't going to ask. Some guys didn't like to be reminded of their time there. Last thing he wanted to do was bring it up and get on Gwilly's bad side, too. Bad enough having Darby mad at him.

Zane looked over his shoulder. "What are you researching?"

He couldn't cover it up, so he told him. "The chick we arrested, I knew her when I was a kid. I was just looking up her arrest record."

"Coulda looked that up in the car," Gwilly said.

"Yeah, I didn't think about it," Jake lied.

He leaned in closer. "Kim Vega. She's a regular 'round these parts. Soliciting, resisting, assault on an officer, you name it. I don't even have to look at the list. I've arrested her at least four times in the last five years."

"I don't see any drug charges, though. And she's definitely a junkie." Jake kept scrolling.

"Those charges get dropped when they help us out," Zane half-smiled.

"She's a narc?" He wanted to be surprised, but wasn't.

"She's just looking out for herself. Problem is, there comes a point where she has nothing more to give in return for the charges. She's about at that point now. She's going to be transported to the jail to await trial, and she'll stay there this time, because I bet your bottom dollar she doesn't have money to make bail, and definitely doesn't have collateral."

"What about family?"

"As in parents? She's your age, Jake, she shouldn't need her parents. She's been on this road for a very long time. Some of those theft charges you see? She broke into her grandmother's house and robbed her. I'm sure that family washed their hands of her a long time ago."

"What happened to her?" He knew everything else, Jake assumed he'd know this, too.

"Who the hell knows? Life? She's a junkie. If she doesn't go to prison and die there, she'll die on the streets soon. Or end up killing someone. It's a shit life, but they know that before they choose it, and yet they still stick that needle in." He shook his head and walked away.

Jake thought he was callous, but then he probably would feel the same if she hadn't been the girl of his wet dreams as a kid.

He imagined she'd gone to college and become a nurse, doctor or whatever. He hoped she'd met a nice guy. Sometimes he even wished they had crossed paths and maybe ended up together. The crazy thoughts of a teen driven by testosterone.

Jake closed the file and logged off the computer, then went to see if Kate had finished processing Kim.

She locked Kim back in the holding cell as he walked up.

"Outside. Now." She pointed to the prisoner transport door.

Jake walked, she followed. As soon as they were in the parking area, she pointed to the lawn. It was dark, and Jake stood under the streetlamp looking at Kate. The light made her skin look blue.

"What is going on with you? And don't tell me nothing. I saw the way you looked at that girl."

"I knew her once upon a time. That's all." Jake looked at the grass and moved the blades with the toe of his boot.

"Bullshit. There's more and you know it. Don't lie to me, little boy." Kate face turned reddish purple in the light, and she looked as if her head might explode.

"Fine, she was my childhood crush. I'm in shock, that's all." He looked her in the eyes when he responded. Telling the truth was easier, because Kate was the queen of weeding out bullshit.

"Heaven help me." Kate put her hands on her hips.

"I was just in shock at seeing her like that. I don't know why it bothers me so much."

Kate walked around in a small circle, looking up at the light. "If you lived here as a kid, you're going to run into people from your past on a regular basis. Some good, some bad, maybe many bad. And I'm not being negative, I'm being realistic. We don't exactly hang out with the folks of high society in this job. Well, not *that* kind of high society anyway."

Jake appreciated her trying to lighten the moment, but he barely mustered a smile. "I know. And I only spent summers here, you know. But this one hit me hard." Jake couldn't watch her crazy circle walking anymore and looked back to the building. "I guess, one day, I expected we'd end up together. At twelve, I was enamored."

"That's so sweet." Kate stopped walking and stuck her finger down her throat as if to puke. "But you need to shove that to the side. Remove your personal feelings. Someday you might have to arrest your brother, and it'll suck, but you'll do it for the greater good."

"I have a sister."

"You know what I meant." She kicked Jake with her boot.

"Is it wrong that I want to talk to her? To help her?"

Kate stepped in front of Jake and gripped his shoulders. She stopped short of shaking him. "You can't save them unless they want to be saved. And believe me, this girl, she don't want anyone's help."

"You don't know that," Jake argued.

"Officer Underwood, I grew up in the foster system. My mother was a junkie. Believe me, I know a lifetime loser when I see one. And I've seen my share."

"Sure," he said, wondering if she really grew up in the foster system.

"I'm not talking about on the job. I got moved from foster home to foster home, and even though I was a deviant, I never did drugs. But I sure did see my share of foster brothers and sisters get hooked, OD, and even die. And she's one of them, I'm telling you. She's gonna be that OD call we get in the next six months."

"But she's not a foster kid. She had a family." He didn't know why he kept arguing with her.

"Doesn't make a bit of difference. Even the richest, most pampered kids get hooked. And heroin has a powerful pull, my friend. So get over it."

Jake couldn't believe it. No one wanted to live the way Kim was living. Not forever. Not looking forward to anything other than the next fix. And always looking over her shoulder. It had to get old. The paranoia alone would be exhausting.

"Can I at least talk to her?" Jake asked.

"There's no law against you talking to her as a friend, but don't talk to her about tonight. Nothing. Nada. Got it?"

"Yeah, I got it." Jake needed to understand how this

happened to Kim. Something he couldn't explain to Kate.

Hell, he wasn't a bad looking guy, and he'd had his share of girls over the years, but something about Kim stuck with him. Jake could easily say he'd never been in love. He'd heard the words from girls, and that would be the beginning of the end. He had no desire for attachment. He just wanted to get laid. But when he thought about Kim, it was something more.

"But you'll have to wait until she's transported to County. You aren't going to rehash old times on my watch." She looked at her watch. "Speaking of which, I'm going to check and see how Zane is doing with Danny Boyd."

"Boyd? The guy who ran from you?" Jake asked.

"One and the same. They found him hiding in the bushes. Now he's in our house, and I want to have a chat with him."

Chapter 8

Boyd got to stew in a holding cell until his attorney arrived at seven the next morning. Kate watched Jake as he wrote up his reports and filed them. His typing skills sucked, but at least he'd gotten down the exact template the captain wanted for reports fairly quickly.

"Punctuation is important. You don't want people thinking you're an illiterate cop," Kate said.

"I heard you the first three times," Jake said, then looked over his shoulder, smiling.

Half a dozen times, Kate wanted to roll his chair aside and finish the reports herself. Instead, she paced behind him and chewed her fingernails. She wanted to get back out on the streets, so she wouldn't think about Boyd and not being able to talk to him.

When Jake finally finished, she read over his report and made him make a few changes. Then she practically dragged him back out of the station. She should let him drive, but then she'd have too much time to think about Boyd, and how she wanted a confession. He wasn't smart enough to get away with this. If he was, they wouldn't have him in a holding cell.

She had a few of her own reports to write, but they'd have to wait until the end of the shift after her rookie left. And she hoped Boyd's attorney would arrive early.

She dropped everything and trailed behind Zane like a puppy when they moved Boyd to the interview room.

"Is his attorney here?" she asked.

Zane nodded and walked into the interview room.

Kate followed behind him. Like Zane had said, they'd be working this one together. She didn't think she needed to ask permission.

A tall, skinny guy with a mullet, Boyd looked like trouble. Goodness, when did mullets come back in style? Or was it just for the fringe set? Kate wanted to hand him a bottle of shampoo and a pair of scissors, but she worried if she got too close, she might get lice. She shivered at the thought. Then her head started to itch, and she scratched just behind her ear.

Boyd liked to think he was rolling in the big time, but alas, he was less than small time. Small time would soon be doing big time, Kate thought. Little guys like this didn't kill people, not usually anyway. They did lie, cheat, and steal without a second thought, though.

The public defender, Bob Cook, didn't seem happy to be representing Boyd again, and scooted his chair away from him before sitting down. Maybe he was afraid of getting lice, too. Leaning back, with his arms crossed, he looked at Kate, then at Zane, like, "Let's get on with this."

"Daniel Boyd, the current charges against you are; evading, driving while suspended, reckless driving, grand theft auto, and first-degree murder, not to mention the warrant for failure to appear on an earlier charge," Zane read from the file in front of him.

Kate looked over to see he had photos of Marco Lopez ready to show Boyd.

"That's not including the drug charges from the raid last night, which adds possession with intent to distribute," Kate added.

Boyd leaned forward, his hands flat on the table. "Murder? I dunno what you're talking about. You said something about Marco Lopez last night. I been thinking, and I don't know how you think I offed the guy."

"But you knew he was dead?" Kate asked.

"Hell, no, I didn't know. I ain't seen him in weeks. He comes and goes, you know?"

"If you didn't kill him, what were you doing driving his car?" Zane asked.

Boyd shook his head. "I ain't gonna lie to you, I don't even know what kind of car Marco drives. And I don't drive. You know, suspended license and all."

Boyd looked at Bob, who looked bored, but said nothing.

"Danny, you want me to show my chest camera footage to you? I got you fleeing the scene," Kate said.

"Don't mind you showing me your chest, long as you're offering," Boyd winked.

Kate sucked in a breath. She wasn't going to let his sexist remarks get under her skin.

"Better yet, I'll show you my photos." She reached into the file and slid one of the photos of Marco in the trunk across the table, turning it around for Boyd to see upright.

"Recognize this guy?" Zane asked. "You were driving his car when Corporal Darby pulled you over yesterday."

"I told you, man, I wasn't driving no car," Boyd protested too much.

"Cut the crap, Boyd. We know it was you. Your fingerprints were all over the steering wheel, and the driver side door. You can't lie your way out of this one. But, right now, grand theft auto is the least of your worries."

Boyd leaned in close. "That guy's missing part of his head."

No shit, Sherlock, Kate thought.

"That guy is Marco Lopez," Zane said.

He leaned in and got an even closer look, not at all repulsed by the photo. "Well, I'll be. It is." He looked up. "Who done this to him?"

Kate sat up straight, then leaned forward, her hands on the table, mimicking Boyd. "You tell us, Danny. He was in the trunk of the car you were driving when you ran from me."

"I'm not much for running," Boyd said, thinking he was funny.

Zane slammed his hands on the table. "You think this is funny, Boyd? You're here because your fingerprints were all over the car we found Lopez in. And only your fingerprints." He pushed off the table. "We're done here. Call a deputy and have him escorted to County. He can talk to the judge tomorrow."

Boyd waved his hands, clanking the cuffs on the table. "No, wait. Fine. Look, I was in the Kroger parking lot, and I saw this sweet ride. White Mercedes." He looked from Kate to Zane and back. "It was running, I tell you. Like God had put it there for me. And when I checked the door, God unlocked it for me. He wanted me to go for a ride. I didn't check the trunk before I started rolling."

"God just put that car there for you? Like you deserved a Mercedes?" Kate's voice dripped with sarcasm.

"Right? Like he'd been hearing my prayers." Boyd missing the sarcasm altogether.

"So you jacked the car?" Zane said. He looked at Bob, who still hadn't said a word.

The man was scribbling copious notes, though.

"Yeah, fine, I jacked the car. But I was going to bring it back. I just wanted to feel how smooth it rode, you know? I was bringin' it back, I swear."

"Sure you were," Kate said.

Boyd cocked his head and glared at Kate. "Well, if you hadn't been such a hard ass bitch, I'd have taken the car back. But, no, you had to pull me over for a simple California roll."

Bob looked up. "She pulled you over for sushi?"

Boyd looked at him. "What? Who's talking about sushi?"

"California Roll, it's crab, avocado, and cucumber," Bob informed him.

Kate said, "I think he is talking about rolling through a stop sign." She looked at Boyd. "Some idiots think it's legal."

"He did a California roll, all right," Zane said. "He fled the scene and rolled the stolen car."

"Hence the reckless driving." Bob jotted more notes.

"Where were you planning to dump Lopez's body?" Kate asked.

"I hadn't planned on dumping anything. You think I'd have stol…borrowed that car if I knowed a dead body was in the trunk?"

"So, you didn't kill Marco Lopez?" Zane asked.

"I keep tellin' you, I ain't never killed no one. So that means no, I didn't shoot Marco." Danny leaned back and tried to pull his hands off the table. The cuffs caught on the metal bar.

"You didn't kill Marco, you were just moving the body," Kate said.

"No. I told you, I didn't know he was in the car. Whose car was it anyways?"

As if he hadn't already been told.

"The car belonged to Marco," Zane said. "The way

it looks, you killed him, put his body in the trunk, then Corporal Darby ruined your getaway."

"Were my client's fingerprints on the trunk? On the victim?" Bob asked.

In fact, Danny's prints weren't on the trunk. The body was still being processed. They weren't looking for his prints so much as possible hair and fibers. Same with the interior of the trunk.

"Before you go putting my client in the electric chair, maybe you should take a look at the Kroger parking lot video footage," Bob said as he put his notebook in his briefcase and stood up. "You have forty-eight hours to figure it out, and charge my client."

The man was doing his job. It just didn't look like it.

"Innocent until proven guilty," Kate mumbled to herself.

"What?" Zane asked.

"Nothing," Kate said.

"Forty-eight hours? I can't stay in jail for four days. I got business to take care of," Danny said.

Bob, Zane, and Kate exchanged looks, but didn't correct Boyd. Then Bob turned around and walked out the door.

Kate uncuffed Boyd from the table, then recuffed his arms behind his back.

"You fucking ruined my day, bitch." Boyd practically spat the words.

"You call me a bitch again, and I'll ruin more than your day, asshole." Kate jerked hard on his handcuffs, knowing how good that metal felt against bony wrists.

"You still ruined my day," he sulked.

"Yeah, that makes two of us. Now I have to go to Kroger when I want to go home and get some sleep."

Boyd's slouched posture changed as soon as they stepped into the hall. He stood straight, strutting as they walked back to the holding cell. He wanted everyone to know he was a badass. Kate's body shook as she laughed to herself.

Chapter 9

The night dragged on for years. By the time Jake's shift was over, he decided going to the jail to talk to Kim was a bad idea. He wished his mind felt the same way when he woke up later that day. Getting off work at six in the morning made his first day off feel weird.

Rolling over in bed, he picked his phone up off the nightstand to check the time. Noon. He sat up. He could still make it to the courthouse in time to see Kim. He jumped out of bed, fully intending to take a shower and head out the door. Instead, he made himself a cup of coffee and called the court to see if Kim's bail had been set, then drank his coffee as he contemplated his next move. He could go to the jail just to talk to her. Like Kate said, she wasn't going to be making bail any time soon. This would be his chance to sit down and talk to her. Jake chugged the rest of his coffee and headed out.

Driving to the courthouse, he contemplated how

this might affect his job. They couldn't fault him for wanting to help out a friend, could they? He felt he owed Kim somehow. Or was his own guilt at not keeping in touch weighing on him? As if keeping in touch would have made a difference in her life. Somehow, he felt like he'd abandoned her. He hadn't, but maybe he could be that friend who convinced her to get clean.

Driving to the jail, he pulled into the parking space out front and gave himself a moment to change his mind.

Good thing he didn't wait much longer because as he walked up to the jail, Kim walked through the doors, looking dirtier and more disheveled than the night before.

"Hey," was all he could manage as he stopped in front of her. "You made bail."

She looked up. "What do you want?" Her eyes shifted in every direction, as if she was looking for a shooter.

"Do you have a ride?"

"What the fuck do you care?" She tried to walk around him.

Jake sidestepped around in front of her. "I'm here to give you a ride."

"What's wrong with you? You don't know me or anything about me. Why are you stalking me?"

"Kim, it's me, Jake Underwood, remember me?"

She looked at him, her eyes squinting against the sun, and maybe against a headache. "Little Jake?"

He smiled. "Not so little anymore."

"Right."

"My dear girl, what happened to you?"

She crossed her arms over her chest and asked, "What the fuck happened to *you*?"

Ouch, like being a stand-up guy and a cop was a bad thing. "I'm not sure what you mean."

"I mean we were friends, and then you were gone." She looked around the parking lot. When it seemed she didn't find who or what she was looking for, she said. "Are you going to give me a ride or what?"

"Are you hungry?" Jake thought taking her to Lucien's to eat, chat, and catch up, would be a good start.

"Not really. I don't have any money anyway. And I need to get some clean clothes."

He knew by looking up her records she wasn't married and didn't have any children. What he didn't know was whether she had a boyfriend or a place to stay.

"Okay, I can take you to get cleaned up, and I'll buy you lunch." He could feel his enthusiasm for this idea fading fast. "Where do you live?"

"I can't go back there. It's probably crawling with cops still."

"Oh, you live in that house that we raided last night?"

She uncrossed her arms and shoved him away. "That was you last night? I thought you looked familiar. I was so high, I thought maybe I was seeing things.

Well, screw you. I don't want a ride or lunch from no pig."

She again tried to get around Jake. "Let's just say I'm a friend, and forget the cop part."

"No cop is a friend of mine." She sidestepped again, but with less heart in her moves.

"I'm not the enemy, Kim, I promise. Let's go get you some clean clothes and a shower. We can have lunch delivered." He moved to her side and put his arm around her shoulders.

She stiffened and tried to get away, then she leaned into him as if suddenly too tired to stand on her own.

Once he realized she wasn't going to bolt, he removed his arm from her shoulders, not wanting to get that smell on his own clothing. In the car, he wanted to crack the windows for fresh air, but Kim must have smelled her own stink because she rolled her window down first.

"If you're not interested in going shopping, I can loan you some shorts and a T-shirt, and you can wash your clothes at my place."

She stared out the window, not answering. He didn't know how he could keep her from running if they went to the store, so he drove back to his uncle's house. As he pulled into his parking space, he realized he was letting a total stranger into his uncle's house, and into his life. And he still wondered who paid her bail. He'd have to look it up.

Kim sat up higher in the seat and looked around. "This is the lake house. You own this house now?"

Jake shook his head. "I'm living with my uncle. I'm waiting for my apartment to be painted and cleaned. Then I'm going shopping, buying all new furniture and stuff. I can't wait to have a place of my own."

"Your uncle won't mind me taking a shower and using the laundry?" She looked down at herself.

"He's at the restaurant. He won't even know." Or so Jake hoped. Because even though Uncle Tucker was a nice man, Jake wasn't sure how far his kindness went.

They got out of the car, and Jake contemplated where to hide his gun key. The gun was locked in a case when he wasn't working, but the key was on his ring. It wouldn't be difficult to figure out which one it was. He decided to worry about it later. She probably wouldn't be there that long.

Unlocking the house, he opened the door and pointed down the hall to his bedroom. "First door on the left. I have a full bathroom in my bedroom. Just toss your clothes out, and I'll put them in the washer after you're done with your shower."

For the first time, Jake noticed how old Uncle Tucker's house looked. Nothing had been updated since he was a kid. Same dark wood paneling, same shag carpet. At least he'd had linoleum on the floors of the door leading to the lake, so the carpets didn't have the musty stench he smelled in the lake houses he looked at when he was thinking he could afford to buy a house. He had quickly given up on that idea.

"After? How'm I gonna have clean clothes when I get out?" She crept down the dark hallway, stopping to glance at the family photos on the wall, straightening one of them.

"If I run the washer while you're in the shower, you'll either have a cold shower, or you'll get scalded." He raised his right brow as if to ask, "You okay with that?"

"I'll put them in the wash myself. I don't want you sniffing my soiled panties." She winked at Jake.

He could only imagine how dirty her underwear was. The thought made Jake ill. Who would even think such a thing? He played along and said, "Gross," then laughed.

"What's gross is that this is the same bedroom you had when we were kids." She sniffed around like the room smelled stale.

"Whatever. It's just temporary. It's not *my* room, it's the guest room." Jake opened the closet and grabbed a towel. Tossing it to her, he said, "Everything you need is in the shower. I'll grab you a washrag."

She snagged the towel and shut the bathroom door behind her. Jake went into the linen closet, grabbed a couple of washrags and another bath towel, in case she needed one for her hair. He smiled to himself. She remembered the room.

When he turned around to go back into the bedroom, Kim stood in the doorway, wrapped only in a towel. "I'm not letting you touch my clothes while they stink. Where is the washer?"

"Follow me." He walked in front of her to not look at her, because even though she was scrawny and dirty, she was sexy as hell in that towel. He couldn't afford to think of her that way. But then he thought of her that way when he was twelve, so how was this different?

Kim padded along the hardwood floors in her bare feet. He could hear her steps behind him. "This place hasn't changed much in all of these years. We had a lot of fun, didn't we?"

Jake turned to look at her as they entered the laundry room off the kitchen. He tried to hide the sadness in his heart. "We did. Where did it all go wrong?"

Kim's face turned to stone. She put her clothes in the washer and said, "Don't turn this on while I'm in the shower."

She grabbed the towels from his hand, turned on her heel, and stalked back to the bedroom with purpose. Jake didn't move, just listened to the sound of her feet hitting the floor. Then he pulled his phone from his pocket and ordered pizza.

He had no idea how long he'd been standing in the kitchen, staring out at the lake, when he heard his name. This prompted him to start the washing machine, then look down the hall.

"Jake! Hey, I need clothes." She walked out into the hallway.

Wrapped in the same towel from before her shower, hair twisted up in the other towel. she looked small, sweet, and innocent. The only thing ruining the image was the slight tremors from coming down off drugs. He'd noticed, that even though she probably used meth as her drug of choice, her teeth weren't rotted.

"Sorry, let me start the washer, and I'll grab you some sweat pants and a shirt." He poured detergent in the washer and started it. She stared at him the whole time.

"Don't suppose you have a sports bra in here somewhere? Maybe your aunt?"

"No aunt, just my uncle, and I sincerely doubt he has a sports bra. Though a man bra might not be a bad idea for him." Jake chuckled as he scooted past her in the hall.

His shoulder rubbed against the towel on her breast as he walked by. He'd had plenty of clearance as he passed, but the feel of it shocked and enticed him. He tried to pretend it didn't.

Digging around in the dresser for clothes, he pulled out a pair of drawstring sweatpants that Kim would swim in, and a crew-neck tee. When he turned around to hand them to her, she dropped both of her towels to the floor.

The smile on her face didn't reach her eyes. This was a performance and he could see this wasn't what she wanted. As much as he wanted her, at least the memory of her, he didn't want it like this. Though the thought of pressing his naked body against hers almost made him give in.

"This is what you want, isn't it? It's why you brought me here instead of taking me home. You wanted to clean me up and fuck me?" She raised her arms and spread them wide, her breasts lifting a little as she moved her arms higher.

He couldn't help but take in her thin frame and shaking arms. For an addict, she still had a nice set of firm, round tits, but he tried not to look there, or at her light brown bush at the top of her legs. He felt an involuntary stirring in his crotch.

"No," Jake threw the clothes at her. "I brought you here to help you. Get you cleaned up, and hopefully not with just a shower. But apparently, you aren't ready to get clean. So, put these on and as soon as your clothes are washed and dried, I'll take you wherever you want to go."

As she bent over to pick up the shirt she dropped, Jake saw tears brimming in her eyes. He wasn't going to show empathy. She was a junkie, and she knew how to manipulate people. Standing naked in front of him, he knew she'd have sex with him for money. Manipulation. Hell, it's what junkies did for a living.

"I'm sorry, but everyone wants something from me. No one ever just gives me anything. It's not the way my life works." She pushed her leg into the too long sweatpants while she held the shirt over her chest.

Jake turned back to the dresser and closed the drawers slowly, giving her time to get dressed before turning back around. It took everything in him not to pull the clothes right back off her to grasp her breasts and caress her bare skin. The urge to run soft kisses over her skin overwhelmed him, and he could almost feel her skin on his lips.

The doorbell rang, and Jake sprinted out of the room. What had he gotten himself into?

Opening the door, Jake paid the pizza guy, took the box, and turned around, almost plowing Kim over.

"You're sorry you did this, aren't you? It was a fantasy, and I'm not the girl you remember." She took the pizza box from him. "That TV in your bedroom work?"

Jake nodded. He avoided answering her first question, because the nod was for both the TV and his actions.

"Let's go lay on the bed and eat pizza and watch a movie."

"It's the middle of the day. Wouldn't you rather eat outside?"

"I'm coming down off a week long high, Jake. I want to eat, because I haven't eaten in days, and I want to sleep. Is it okay if I sleep in your bed?" She nudged him with her elbow.

Being on the same bed with her wasn't a good idea, but Jake was hungry and tired, too. He let her take the pizza and lead the way, enjoying watching her walk down the hall in front of him. Enjoying seeing her in his baggy clothes.

Chapter 10

Before Kate left the station, she checked with CID for any new evidence from the trunk of Lopez's car. She drove home disappointed. So far, the only evidence Boyd left behind were his prints on the driver side door and the interior driver side. While Kate checked on the evidence, Zane called the manager at Kroger.

She should be point on the investigation. She'd been trying to get off patrol and into CID for months. She hoped training Jake and getting her promotion to sergeant would expedite the process, not keep her in patrol. The department was short on patrol officers, so even though they'd need her to investigate, she'd still continue to patrol. Not that she didn't like being a patrol officer; she loved it, but she wanted more.

"Gotta love franchises. They need a warrant to get the video, and even then, it could take a few days for Kroger to get the files from the corporate office." Zane explained to Kate as she walked down the hall.

Whatever, as long as she didn't have to release Boyd.

She wouldn't be releasing him anyway. He'd go in front of the judge for the other charges even if she didn't get the murder charge to stick. And with what he had on his sheet, she doubted the judge would set a low bail.

As soon as she got to her car, she picked up her phone and called Victor Norris' office.

"Yes, Miss Kate, he's still planning to meet you at eleven. Is that still going to work with your schedule?" Miss Eva's voice as sweet as apple pie.

"I'm good, thanks," Kate lied. She wanted to go home and sleep until the next morning.

She disconnected, then immediately called Bryce Trident. She'd known Bryce for as long as she could remember. They'd met in foster care. He'd seen his share of abusive homes before ending up living with Kate's foster parents at the age of twelve.

That was when Kate thought Bryce was gay, even though she didn't really know what it meant. Once when they were playing with their Barbie and Ken dolls, she tried to kiss him, and he shoved her so hard she fell over backwards. That's when she saw he had her Ken doll on top of his Ken doll, only one was behind the other. She never tried to kiss him again, and she never played with Barbie dolls around him, either. And when he left that day, she gave Ken a bath because she didn't want Barbie to be mad at him. As it turned out, Bryce wasn't gay, but he'd been abused. Abused in ways another human being should never have to endure. Many times over the years, she wondered if he was trying to tell her something, but she was too young to understand at the time.

When they were foster siblings, and in high school, Bryce brought a girl to the house, and Kate actually said out loud, in front of the girl, "I thought you were gay." Yep, that went over well. She never saw the girl at the house again. Bryce didn't seem at all offended by her statement, and even laughed.

"If she's that sensitive, I don't want her for my girlfriend," he said, then went to his bedroom and shut the door.

It was the last time Bryce brought a girl home.

"What are you doing in an hour?"

She heard a yawn, and what sounded like stretching. "Sleeping."

"It's almost ten o'clock," Kate said. "Get up and take a shower. I'm picking you up in forty-five minutes."

Sounding no more awake, Bryce said, "No, you're not. I'm hanging up now."

"If you aren't ready, I'll drag you to my new house dressed in just your boxers."

Definitely more awake now. "New house? You didn't tell me you were house hunting. Now I'm pissed."

"I wasn't. And you know I wouldn't look at houses without you. I'll tell you all about it when I pick you up.

Now go shower. I'm on my way home to take a shower myself. See you in a few."

Kate smiled as she put her phone in the cup holder of the center console. Times like this were for sharing with best friends. Or in this case, her sort of brother and best friend.

Unlike Kate, Bryce had gone off the deep end. Drugs took over his life. The same vice that put him in foster care would be his demise. It made Kate sad, but she knew nothing she said or did would change his addiction. Eventually, he'd get clean or die.

Not that Kate was innocent by any means; she had her own vices, but not drugs, she'd never go there. She had her share of drunken stupors and one nights stands. In fact, before she married Zane, she preferred one-night stands. No ties, no messiness. She didn't have to explain herself, and didn't want to know anything about the guy she just had sex with. In fact, she preferred the walk of shame, because she sure wasn't taking them back to her place. Then they'd know where she lived. Only once did she see a guy she'd had sex with and later go up and talk to him. Usually she pretended she had no idea who they were if she ran into them again.

Bryce liked his one nighters, too. Only he was stupid enough to bring them back to his place, which happened to be where Kate lived too, at the time. Kate intervened a few times to keep Bryce from going down a rabbit hole. Bryce was a whore, and she loved him for it, because he'd traded in drugs for sex. She'd rather see his nightstand full of condoms than needles. They both had their issues, but they also had each other.

In recent years, Bryce slowed a little. Not because he was getting older, Kate suspected, but because he was getting wiser, and maybe even ready to settle down. She doubted that would last long. Bryce had been a free bird for too long, just like her. The scars of his past might never heal, and she knew it, so she wanted to be sure she was there for him. And even though her scars didn't run as deep, and she'd escaped the brutality of being sexually molested, she understood Bryce's behavior as if she had been.

Showered, dressed in faded blue jeans and a thin white tee over a pink camisole, Kate pulled her car up to the curb outside Bryce's apartment complex. The gray brick building looked cheery with its white window boxes, all planted with some sort of pink and red flowers. Kate had no idea what they were, just that it was a good thing they had a landscape management company keeping them watered and fertilized, because if it were up to Bryce, the plants would be dead.

She checked her phone to see if she'd missed a message from Bryce before honking her horn. She looked at his apartment door, waiting for movement. None. She swiped her phone and called his number. It rang three times and went to voicemail.

"Jerk," she said to the phone. When she looked up, she saw Bryce pulling his apartment door closed behind him.

Dress in plaid cotton shorts and a skin-tight baby blue tee, she could see every muscle on his scrawny upper body. Drugs had done their number on Bryce, but he tried to compensate by working out regularly. He'd never be in a body building contest, but he was lean and fit like a runner. She always thought his curly mop of red hair made him look perpetually fifteen years old. He always got carded when they went out drinking.

She rolled down the window to tell him to hurry up, and could hear his flip-flops on the sidewalk.

"Really? Flip-flops? We're going to a really nice place," Kate said.

"It's your new house, how nice can it be? You're a cop, for God's sake." Bryce climbed into her car and immediately pulled his phone from his pocket.

Most people would think Bryce rude, but Kate didn't care that Bryce preferred his phone to conversation with her. Most of the time.

"I'm investigating a murder," she said.

"Uh-huh," Bryce said.

Kate shoved him. He shoved her back.

"Did you hear me? I'm investigating a murder."

Bryce looked at her. "Sure, you are."

"If you put your damn phone down for half a second, I'll tell you about it."

Bryce dropped his phone in his lap. "This better be good. I was texting with Joey."

Joey worked at the same hospital Bryce did, and they were best buddies. Always texting if they weren't hanging out. They met in medical school. And even though Bryce hadn't finished medical school, he continued his path to a career in medicine and became a nurse.

Kate told Bryce about the driver who took off, the accident, and the body in the trunk. The entire time, Bryce stared at her with his mouth open. She was sure he thought she had made it all up.

When she finished, he said, "Yeah, okay, so who was the driver?"

Kate shrugged. "That I can't tell you just yet. It's an ongoing investigation."

"Did the driver kill the guy in the trunk?"

"I can't say," she said.

Bryce groaned. "Then why did you even bother to tell me?"

Kate steered onto the ramp to I-30, heading east. "I'm excited. It's my first murder. And if this goes well, I might get to be full time CID."

"I've heard that before. You'll be a grandma before you ever get off patrol." He picked his phone back up. "Where're we going anyway? Louisiana?"

"Didn't they deliver the guy to your morgue?" Kate asked.

"Might have. I've had a few days off. I went on a bender with Joey. His last, you know."

Kate glanced at Bryce. "What do you mean? Is he going into treatment or something?"

Bryce grimaced. "He's getting married, and you know how it is. The girl is already jealous of the time we spend together. When he marries her, I'll be persona non grata."

"No way. I'll bet she loves you as much as Joey. Besides, you're like a mother-in-law; part of the package."

"Mother-in-law? Thanks."

Kate drove a few miles, then exited the interstate, turning left. She drove another three miles when she saw it on the right side of the road. Her new farm.

"You got a hankerin' for pecans?" Bryce turned up the twang.

"This is my new house." Kate turned her car into the driveway.

Bryce threw his head back and laughed. "Good joke." Then he stopped laughing. "I can't believe you got me out of bed to pull a prank."

Kate stopped the car, leaning forward to get a closer look. "Not a joke. Apparently, I had a rich grandfather, and he left this place to me."

Bryce's head lolled to the right, as if he'd gone to sleep.

Kate told the story of her morning at the attorney's office as she rolled up to the Lexus convertible parked in the circular driveway.

"Then you might want to get a real estate agent, because you can't afford this place. And you know nothing about growing and harvesting pecans."

She didn't even bother to repeat the part about the trust.

She parked behind the Lexus and got out of the

car, not looking back to see if Bryce planned to join her. As she walked up to the Lexus, the front door of the home opened.

"Good morning, Miss Darby. I'm so glad you could make it." Victor looked at his watch as if she were late.

She looked at her own watch. 10:55. "I'm excited and nervous."

Victor stepped out onto the porch. "Nothing to be nervous about."

Kate turned in a circle, taking it all in. To the left of the house; acres and acres of pecan trees stretched further than she could see. To the right, it looked like acres of grass hay. And the building in front of her, an antebellum southern home.

The stark white box-style mansion looked like it belonged in Georgia, with its balcony running the length of the outside edge of the home. Enormous pillars stretched from the ground to the roof, and evenly spaced large windows graced either side of the enormous entrance.

Kate noticed the balcony of the second floor acted as shade for the first floor porch, which also stretched the length of the front of the house. A border of perfectly manicured boxwoods grew along the outside of the deck, along with small, but colorful flowering bushes.

She walked toward the house and ascended the steps of the porch. Victor greeted her at the edge of the steps and shook her hand. "This is the most recent incarnation of the home. And it's about four times the size of the original structure."

"Wow. This is a lot of space for one person," Kate marveled at the twin wooden rocking chairs swaying lightly in the breeze.

"It's a beautiful space. I'm not sure if I mentioned, you'll have a weekly cleaning service. It usually takes her eight hours to clean. If she needs more time, like she's cleaning windows, she'll come back a second day. Make sure you let her know what time works for you. Right now, she's coming on Mondays at seven in the morning."

Kate smiled at the idea of having a cleaning service. "That's perfect. She can keep the same schedule."

"Let's go inside, then I'll show you around the gardens." Victor turned and walked back to the front doors.

Kate stepped in behind him, and the sight nearly took her breath away. She felt as if she'd stepped into a smaller version of Tara from *Gone with the Wind*.

She'd been in the plantation homes in Louisiana, and they looked practical, not like the plantation homes of *Gone with the Wind*. Small bedrooms, small everything. It was about practicality, not audacity. She had expected the same of this house, until she pulled into the driveway.

The enormous foyer was flanked on both sides with sweeping stairways, both leading to a landing which filled the expanse on the second floor. When she looked up, the light off the crystal chandelier caught her eye.

"This is so not my style," she whispered, "but I could get used to it."

"You'll have to. You can't change anything. Not even the interior of the master bedroom, which I assume will be yours."

"I guess I'll learn to live with it," Kate said.

Victor smiled. "The family didn't want to entertain, so there aren't any grand ballrooms or anything, but the dining room and parlor are quite nice. And a kitchen was added to the main house about twenty years ago."

Kate frowned at Victor. "What do you mean? They didn't have a kitchen?"

"Most of the older grand homes didn't have the kitchen attached to the house. There was a great fear of fire. In fact, the kitchen in this house burned to the ground twice."

Kate's eyes went wide.

Victor smiled. "That was almost a hundred years ago. I promise the current kitchen is all upgraded and safe."

He waved his arm, and Kate followed. Before they stepped out of the foyer, Kate heard footsteps behind her on the wood floor and turned to see Bryce.

He looked like a little boy in a huge toy store who didn't know where to go first.

"What do you think?" Kate asked.

Bryce gazed around the space, his mouth open in awe, his eyes wide. *"As God as my witness, I will never be hungry again."*

"That was my first thought, too."

Chapter 11

The empty pizza box sat at the foot of the bed at eleven in the evening when Jake awoke. The pizza box there, Kim gone. He bolted up in bed.

"Damn it." Jake got up to go to the bathroom, then walked down the hall to grab a bottle of water from the refrigerator.

Kim and Tucker sat at the kitchen table with the coffee pot on the warmer in the middle between them. Each had their hands wrapped around a coffee mug.

He walked in on them as quietly as possible, so they didn't turn around.

"That feels like forever ago," Kim's voice sounded sad.

"In a way, it was a lifetime ago. I'm sorry you've had it rough, but it's your own fault for making bad decisions." Tucker took another sip of coffee.

Leave it to Tucker to not sugar coat the truth. Jake waited for Kim to cross her arms in front of her, or get up and storm out. She surprised him by putting her hand on Tucker's forearm, and saying, "You're right. I took what I thought was the easy way out. Turns out it was the toughest road I coulda traveled. And now I got no idea how to get back to where I need to be."

Tucker looked at Kim and said, "You don't need to go back. You need to take a hard right, and get off this path of destruction. It's your decision to make, and you'll make it when you're good and ready. I just wish your parents were here to help you get on track."

"I miss them every day, but I have no excuses. I messed up and they aren't interested in my bullshit anymore. Tucker, I'm in a shitload of trouble. I don't want Jake to go down with me, but he picked me up from the jail, and now I don't know how to tell him he made a huge mistake." She took a long sip of coffee, then put the mug on the table and crossed her arms.

"Then don't. Just leave. He's not in deep. He just picked you up, that's it. Gave you a ride, a shower, clean clothes, and a few hours of much needed sleep. You tell me where you need to go, and I'll take you there." Tucker stood and grabbed the coffee pot off the table.

Jake jumped back around the corner, so he wouldn't be seen.

He knew this was a mistake, and he was just glad Kim hadn't robbed them blind while he was sleeping. At least not that he knew of at this point. And Tucker. What would he have done if that had happened? Family heirlooms can't be replaced, and somehow Jake felt that's what she would have taken. She still might. Or maybe not.

From the kitchen sink, where Tucker poured the rest of the coffee in his cup, he said, "Let's go. I'll take you anywhere you need to go."

"I don't want to make Jake mad." Kim didn't sound like she really cared all that much.

"Don't worry about Jake. He's a big boy, and he'll be fine. Change your clothes, and I'll get the car keys. We'll be out of here before Jake even realizes you're out of bed."

Jake rushed back to the bedroom, not wanting his uncle to know he was eavesdropping. He climbed in bed and closed his eyes. Then he waited for Kim or Uncle Tucker to enter the room. He listened for any sounds coming down the hallway.

Kim didn't come into the room, and a few minutes later, Jake heard two car doors slam, then his uncle's car start. He willed himself to sleep as he heard the car drive away. Sleep didn't come easily. Just when he drifted off, he heard his uncle's car again, and the back door slamming. He laid on his back with his hands behind his head and listened to the sounds of his uncle preparing for bed.

Jake awoke around seven, pissed off and grumpy. His mood had less to do with Kim leaving than how she snuck away in the middle of the night without so much as a thank you. She probably did him a favor. At least he tried to look at it that way. He mentally kicked himself for possibly putting his job on the line for her, only for her to basically spit in his face.

"Morning," Uncle Tucker said. "I met your house-guest last night."

"Oh?" He didn't want to admit he heard them, and knew what happened.

"We had coffee last night. Then she needed a ride, so I took her where she wanted to go." He opened the cabinet and pulled out the canister of coffee.

Jake grabbed the pot from the coffee machine and filled it with filtered water from the faucet. "Where'd she want to go?"

"Home, apparently. At least that's what she said."

Jake poured the water into the machine. "Okay. Well, thanks."

"Next time you want to invite a junkie into my house, I'd appreciate you talking to me about it first." He carefully measured out the grounds into the filter and pushed it into place, then he pushed the brew button. Jake heard no malice in his words, no warning, just relaying his expectations.

"I'm sorry. I was just going to get her something to eat, and some clean clothes. We fell asleep watching TV."

He shook his head. "You're a cop. You should know better than to let a junkie in your home unsupervised."

He damn sure knew better, and didn't feel like being lectured. He already felt stupid enough for even offering to help.

"Did you check your wallet, your dresser stash, or

anywhere else you hide money? Make sure she didn't rob you blind?"

Jake shook his head.

"You're smarter than this, boy."

Jake's cell phone danced across the kitchen counter.

"I've gotta grab this. It might be work." He snatched the phone up, knowing good and well it wasn't work, and walked out to the porch.

The morning air still and hot, he could smell the lake in the air. He took a deep breath and swiped his phone screen.

"Underwood?"

What do you know? It was work. "Yeah," Jake replied.

"You need to come down to the station and pick up your girlfriend," Kate snapped.

"What are you talking about? I don't have a girlfriend."

"Kim Vega." The words couldn't have sounded more clipped.

"What the hell?"

"She says you're her boyfriend, and she'd like you to come pick her up. Jake, we need to have a talk. Get here ten minutes ago." Kate hung up before Jake could respond.

He must have looked worried or scared, because when he walked back into the kitchen his uncle asked, "Are you okay?"

"Too weird, but that was work."

"How is that weird? You just said it probably was."

Tucker smeared about a pound of butter on his rye toast.

"Never mind. I have to go in." Jake grabbed his car keys from the hook, slipped into his sandals by the back door, and walked out.

Kate stood outside the station as Jake drove up. She marched up to his car and opened the door before he could even put it in park.

"What the hell are you doing?"

"Before you start jumping all over me, could you please tell me what's going on?" He got out and stood close to the door, just in case he had to make a run for it. Kate scared the crap out of him.

"You're shacking up with a suspect in our drug case?" She grabbed Jake by the chin with one hand and squeezed. "Don't you like being a cop?"

"I love being a cop, but that's beside the point. Are you going to tell me why you called me to come pick her up? What's she doing here, and how does it have anything to do with me?"

As if her energy had been drained, Kate sat on the curb. Stepping away from the car, Jake closed the door. It felt weird to be looking down at her, but he didn't dare sit next to her.

"She came to the station early this morning. She stayed in the waiting area until I arrived. Said she'd only talk to me." Kate shook her head. "It's my day off too, you know."

"I know."

"She had a story to tell. She wants out. She wants help. She decided to snitch out her housemates in order to get into the S.A.F.E program. Kim's no dummy. She knows the system well. Said she wanted to talk to the D.A., but only if she could do it today, and only if he'd give her the deal."

"It's Saturday morning. The D.A. isn't going to come in on a Saturday." Jake felt too tired mentally and suddenly physically to stand and sat next to Kate. Seeing Kim again turned out to be more than he bargained for.

"He's here right now. He's been here about an hour."

Jake looked at his watch. It was just after eight. "She must have some good shit, huh?"

"You have no idea." Kate rocked back and forth. "And this is the part you're going to love…" she hesitated, then just stopped talking.

"What, Kate? What did she say?"

"It's more about what D.A. Anderson said." She now picked at the seam on her jeans.

"Corporal Darby, please tell me what's going on." Jake realized Kate wasn't his friend in this, she was his trainer and his boss.

"Well, Officer Underwood," the disdain in her voice thick, "You're going to have custody of her until the trial. And she'll be remanded to you after she sees the judge on Monday."

"Is she in custody?" Jake asked.

"No, she made bail, remember? You picked her up, or did you forget already that you're knee deep in this?"

Oh, shit, Jake had really rolled in it this time. "But I was just giving her a ride home from the jail. She looked lost when she walked out, and I asked her if she needed a ride."

She looked him in the eyes. "And what the hell were you doing at the jail to begin with? And don't tell me it was work related. I hate liars."

Jake looked at the ground. "I went to see her."

"You foolish little boy." She stood. "You've stuck your foot in it all the way to your ankle, so now you're stuck with her for the duration of the S.A.F.E. program, or until she's back in jail."

"I can't be responsible for her. I can barely take care of myself." He ran his fingers through his short hair.

"Now you have the equivalent of a small child. She'll have to check in with the judge at least once a week and be piss tested daily. And she's all yours." She leaned down and grabbed Jake's hand. "Come on, the D.A. wants to have a chat with you."

Jake felt ill as he thought about how he was going to explain this to his uncle.

S.A.F.E program stood for Stop Addiction For Ever, and it was what the D.A. agreed to in lieu of dropping all of the charges. Kim would plead no contest to the charges and start the program right away. This all came after a long sit down with D.A. Anderson and Sergeant Gwilly.

"Start naming names, Miss Vega, or I'm not going to be able to help," Anderson said.

Kim took a long drink from her water bottle. "I already told you."

Kim said she knew the who, what, when and where of a major drug buy going down within the next two weeks. She'd sign the deal, and give up names, places, and transaction details. Anderson grinned so big, Jake could barely see the rest of his face when they sat down together.

Kim sat quietly on the far side of the table, not looking at Jake as D.A. Anderson spoke to him.

"She says you're her rock, so you should know, you'd better be Stonehenge unmovable on this," Anderson said.

"Her rock?" Jake said. "I barely know her."

He looked at Kim. She looked down.

"The S.A.F.E program is the only way she gets to stay out of prison. And she knows it. I've already explained the details of the program to Kim. Do I need to explain it all to you, too?"

Jake shook his head. He'd heard about the program from Kate. It could work, but the person had to want to get clean.

Anderson explained it anyway.

Kate hadn't been joking. Kim would be drug tested daily, and she'd have to meet with the judge a minimum of once a week in the beginning, and every other week after she graduated to the next steps in the program. If she broke the rules, she'd be remanded to prison to serve out the full sentence of her felony charge. If she stayed clean and graduated out of the program, she'd have the felony removed. But she had to be under a sort of house arrest, and needed someone to answer for her. She gave them Jake Underwood's name.

Uncle Tucker was going to freak, Jake knew it, and his fingers trembled as he dialed his number.

"Uncle Tucker?" Jake's voice cracked.

"Yes, she can stay with us." He didn't even wait for Jake to ask, or hesitate.

"What? How did…?"

"I had a long talk with that girl last night. Then on the way home she asked me what I'd do if I were her. I told her I'd leave that life behind." He sighed. "I asked if she wanted me to stay with her, but she declined. I suspected she wasn't going to follow through on what she told me she *should* do. It takes a lot of guts to give up everyone you know and start over. It's the hardest part of addiction. All of your friends are addicts, and they want you to be the same as them, they pressure you, so you fall back." A pause. "Maybe together, we can keep her from falling back."

Jake breathed a sigh of relief. Uncle Tucker being on board would make it easier. Not that he'd ask him for anything, but at least he wouldn't have to lie. He hated even lying by omission. "Thanks, Uncle Tucker."

"Don't thank me. I may have just made your life a living hell. And I have no intentions of throwing you a lifeline when you start drowning. Call this a life lesson." He hung up the phone.

The paperwork signed, Jake Underwood was now the guardian for Kim Vega. It would've been nice for her to ask his permission first, but who was he kidding? He'd have agreed to nearly anything if it would get her clean and back to the sweet Kim he remembered from childhood.

They say you can never go back, and as Kim sat beside him in the car, her arms crossed, not saying a word, Jake realized there was the equivalent of the Berlin Wall between them. She didn't want help; she just wanted out. She wanted to be free, not in prison, or jail. Jake was her "get out of jail free" card. And in his ignorance, he thought she'd be grateful. Thought she'd be happy to have help getting clean.

"Don't judge me," were her first words.

Jake didn't respond.

"You don't have any idea what my life has been like since the accident."

He looked at her, and a tear rolled down her cheek. Afraid to let his guard down because he didn't know what was real and what was a lie. "What accident?"

"The accident that killed my family. I wish I'd been killed that day." The tears were coming faster, and dripping onto her crossed arms.

Wanting to slam on the brakes, pull off to the side of the road, and just listen, Jake felt conflicted at not believing her. It was the first time she'd offered to share anything about her life, or her past. He didn't know if he should ask for details. "Is that what you and Uncle Tucker were talking about last night?"

"Yeah. He was the one called 911 that day. It happened in front of his restaurant." She dropped her arms to her sides.

"I never heard about this."

"I don't think we had been to the lake house for a few years when it happened. A drunk driver came flying around the curve. You know that one north of Lucien's?"

Jake knew it. He also knew of one other accident when a car lost control on the wet road and slammed into the restaurant sign. The guy had been drunk, got out of the car, and walked about half a mile away. They found him dead on someone's front lawn. Sad part was that if he'd had stayed at the car, the paramedics could have saved his life. If he hadn't been driving drunk, he'd still be alive, Jake reminded himself. "I know which curve you're talking about."

"It was raining hard. Anyway, he lost control of the car in the turn, and it started spinning. The cops called it hydroplaning. His car slammed into the driver's side of my parents' car, then flipped over the top of it, crushing us. My parents died at the scene and my sister died a week later. I survived with a minor fracture of the vertebrae in my back. Lots of pain, but I didn't have any spinal damage. Just lots of pain, both physical and mental."

"Back pain is debilitating enough without the pain of losing your family." He wondered why he never heard about the accident. Wondered why Uncle Tucker never told him.

"I went to live with my grandmother. She didn't want a teenage girl in her house. She blamed me for the accident because I'd been the one who wanted to go to Arlington for the weekend. Six Flags, you know? Anyway, my grandmother had a few bad habits she shared with me. I went from an addiction to her prescription pain meds to illegal meds, and then I went hard after she died. I've been an addict since I was sixteen." She turned and looked at Jake. "Not how I thought my life would go."

"My boss said one of your arrests was for robbing your grandmother. Is that true?"

Kim looked out the window. "I did a lot of things I'm not proud of. And I'll probably screw up a few more times before it's over."

He could feel her looking at him now, but he stared straight ahead at the road, navigating the narrow streets near the lake house. "I'm so sorry we lost touch."

He thought about the conversation Kim had with his uncle. She said her family had written her off. And it didn't seem like she'd been talking about her grandmother, it seemed as if she'd been talking about her parents. He wanted to ask Tucker about the accident, but it would have to wait until Kim couldn't hear. He didn't want her to think he didn't believe her. Not a good start to this guardian relationship.

"Me too. Somehow, I think things may have been different if we still had the lake house. Still had the old friends. My grandma's neighborhood, the trailer park, didn't have the greatest influences. And I was weak."

"We're all weak in one way or another." Jake realized in that statement she was his weakness. "I'll do my best to be strong for you, Kim, but I don't know if I'm up to the task. And I can't let this interfere with my uncle's life, either. We'll have to work out some rules."

She reached across and grabbed his hand, lacing her fingers in his and said, "Thank you. If you hadn't come to get me yesterday, I don't think I'd have come to this decision. It's been so long since I've seen how other people live. I forgot that life. Being with you and talking to your uncle, I know I want more." She gripped his hand hard. "I don't want to die in prison."

Jake squeezed back. He had no words.

"I know everyone is expecting me to fail, but I'm telling you, I won't. That Darby cop hates me. I can see it in her eyes. She thinks I'm going to bring you down." She tried to let go of Jake's hand.

He held fast. "Kate just knows how real life works. She's been a cop for a long time. She's a good lady. When you prove that you're serious about changing, she'll come around."

Oh, God, Kate was never going to let him live this down if Kim reoffended. He didn't think he could handle the disappointment in her eyes when Kim got carted back to jail. Yes, she was his senior officer, and no, he didn't have a thing for her, but he did want her to be proud of his decision to intervene.

Tucker had put on a fresh pot of coffee, and left a note beside it.

Had to go to the restaurant. Kim will need a job, so I expect

to see her at Lucien's at 4:30pm sharp, so we can do the paper-
work and start training. Clean the coffee pot when you're finished,
and load the dishwasher. We'll discuss more chores tomorrow.

Love,

Uncle Tucker

"He's a good man, you're lucky to have him." Kim
opened the cabinet and pulled down two cups. "This is
about as much of a drug as I'll be able to have from
now on," she grinned.

Jake held up his hand. "I'm good for now. I need to
go take a shower and think."

She stepped in close and stood on her tiptoes,
kissing him on the cheek.

Not knowing what to say, or how he felt, Jake just
turned around and walked out of the room.

The hot shower should have been a cold shower,
because all he could think of was a future with Kim.
How she'd get clean, and they'd live happily ever after.
He wondered if she wanted kids. He wondered how
great she'd be in bed. He fantasized long enough the
water turned cold. Stepping out of the shower and into
his bedroom, he wiped himself dry with a towel. When
he looked up, Kim was lying on his bed.

"I know you didn't want to do anything last night,
but today is a new day. You didn't pick me up from the
cop shop so you could get laid. But I see you," she
looked Jake's naked body up and down, "and I know
you want me."

Hormonal Jake won out. He went to her, climbed

on top of her, and kissed her like he wanted to since they were kids. "You taste like coffee."

She pulled back. "You taste like toothpaste." Then she pushed hard against him and the kisses were bruising in their need.

Their teeth clicked. She bit him on the ear lobe; he sucked at her bottom lip. He felt as if he hadn't made out with a girl in years. This felt new and primal.

She shook her head and whispered in his ear, "Baby, you have a condom?"

And if that didn't ruin the mood. He didn't have any condoms.

Chapter 12

Both Kate and Zane had come to the station, even though they had the day off. Afterward, they went to Kate's new house. She wanted Zane to see it, get his approval for some reason. Bryce had fallen in love and already had plans to move out of his apartment.

"This place is amazing," Zane said as they walked up the grand stairway to the second floor.

"It's a bit much. I thought about sleeping here last night, but then chickened out. I figured there are probably many ghosts in this place and I couldn't sleep here alone."

"Bryce didn't offer to stay with you?"

Kate turned and glared at Zane. She knew he liked Bryce, but she also knew he hated that she shared more with Bryce than with him. Bryce knew all of her secrets and skeletons, Zane not so much.

"He's making plans to move in," Kate said.

"Isn't it a little far from the hospital?" Zane asked.

"He works in the morgue. It's not like he's going to get a late-night emergency call for a woman in labor."

She felt the urge to reach out and take his hand, but that would lead places neither of them needed to go. Her heart hurt with how much she still loved him and how much she still needed him. But they had to move past that.

"It's crazy how they fit the bathrooms into the layout when you know there weren't bathrooms or indoor plumbing in the original structure." Kate opened the door to a massive bathroom off the upstairs hallway.

"The fixtures are true to the time period. Love the clawfoot tub." Zane walked around the bathroom and as he did, Kate realized the room was larger than her bedroom in her current place.

"Wait until you see the bedrooms. Straight out of a romance novel, I swear."

She showed him all the rooms, but stood in the doorway, not daring to enter a bedroom with him. One of the two of them might make a move they couldn't back away from.

"Victor said these cotton sheers will be replaced with heavy velvet drapery come October or November. They apparently think the sheers are better for keeping the house cool. I think the heavy drapery with closed windows would keep the sun out and be better."

"Before air conditioning, they'd open all the

windows and let the air blow through the house, so I see the point. But it looks like someone installed central air in recent years."

The day hadn't warmed to the point of stifling yet, so it hadn't dawned on Kate that the air conditioning was blowing. She walked over to an ornate metal grate and felt the cool air.

"Let's go sit in the parlor," she said.

Downstairs, Kate and Zane walked into the parlor off the main foyer, only to see a large pitcher of tea and two glasses filled to the top with ice. Kate tensed. Had Bryce stopped by? She moved to the front of the house to look for his car. Nope, just hers and Zane's.

"Shit, there really are ghosts," Kate said.

"I think there's a logical explanation." Zane opened the set of double doors on the back side of the room, which opened to a small dining room.

Beyond the dining room, Kate saw a tall, black woman standing in the kitchen. Who the hell was this? And what was she doing in Kate's house?

Zane walked next to Kate as she entered the kitchen.

"Hi, I'm Kate Darby, and you are?"

The woman had smooth skin the color of black coffee, reddish brown hair, and eyes so dark Kate thought they might be black. But her dark eyes held a sparkle. Kate couldn't place her age, but knew she was older than her skin portrayed. She wore a long floral print skirt that looked light and airy, and a peasant type white cotton shirt.

"Pleased to finally meet you, Miss Kate. Edward has spoken of you often over the years." She didn't offer a hand or her name.

Zane stepped forward, offering his hand. "I'm Zane Gwilly, and you are?"

Still not offering her name, she said, "I'm a tenant on the property."

"Do you have a name?" Kate meant it to come out friendlier than it did.

"Azizi Carter," she said, a hint of Cajun coming through in the pronunciation.

"Miss Azizi, what are you doing in my house?"

"Mr. Victor didn't tell you?" She cocked her head, then turned back to the sink. "I was born and raised here. Lived here all my life. As did my parents, grandparents, and great-grandparents. The Carters are part of the property, you might say."

Kate leaned against the doorframe. "Victor mentioned a tenant, but not one that stayed in the main house."

Azizi laughed. "Oh, no, Miss Kate, I don't live in the main house. I live in the tenant house out back. The only person who ever lived in this house lived in the servant's quarters off the kitchen. That's now a small guest room with a bathroom."

Kate didn't like how the woman didn't directly answer her questions. "But you just come and go as you please from the main house?"

Azizi didn't look at Kate as she nodded. She continued with her hands low in the sink. Kate wanted to step forward to see what the woman was doing. Instead, she said, "Do you have family here, too?"

Azizi looked at Kate now, the sparkle gone from her eyes. "I have no family."

Zane broke the silent tension. "Nice meeting you, Miss Azizi. And thank you for the tea." He took Kate by the wrist and pulled her away from the door. "Let's go enjoy the tea."

"What if it's poisoned?" Kate asked as they sat down. The curtains and windows had been opened to let the breeze flow through the room. Kate felt uneasy. "See? This is why I didn't sleep here last night."

Zane poured tea into both glasses. "I'll taste test for you."

Kate watched as Zane drank down half a glass of tea. "It doesn't have to kill you right away."

"It won't kill you," Azizi said behind them. "It's only spiked with a little hooch."

Kate nearly toppled her glass as she jumped up from her chair. "Do you always sneak around like this?"

Azizi's lips curved only a little. It could have been a smile, but Kate couldn't be sure.

"It's delicious," Zane said. "In fact, I don't think I've ever enjoyed a glass of tea this much. Only now I won't be able to drive home."

Azizi's expression morphed into a full grin with perfect white teeth showing. "Oh, Mr. Zane, it's not a lot of hooch. You be fine."

For the first time, her grammar wasn't perfect. Kate

thought it said a lot about who she was. But what it said, she wasn't yet sure.

Kate dared to take a sip from her glass, then settled back into her chair. "Whoa, this has a bite. It's delicious."

Azizi turned to walk away. "Been in my family for generations. Glad you like."

Kate felt bad for being so bitchy. "Won't you join us?"

"It's not proper. Enjoy. I'll have lunch ready around one."

Kate jumped up again. "No, Miss Azizi, you don't need to cook for me."

Azizi didn't respond.

Kate thought about following her back to the kitchen, but decided to sit back down.

"Do you think she worked for my grandfather?" she asked.

Zane looked at her, his face questioning. "And I would know this how?"

She wanted to smack him, but sipped her tea instead. "What do you think about this whole thing with the Vega chick and Underwood?"

"I'm trying not to think about it," Zane stood and walked to the window. "What a view."

"That little Angry Betty is up to something. I can't quite put my finger on it. But she's not on the up and up. And now she's dragged my officer into her quagmire."

"Really? Quagmire?"

"It means—"

"I know what it means. Just a weird word choice." He put his glass back on the table. "I've got to get home to Wally."

"How's Wally doing?"

"He misses you," Zane said.

"That's bullshit, Zane, he's always been your dog."

Wally had been Zane's gift to her, but the dog, a red merle Australian Shepherd, had fallen hard for Zane from day one. He'd never been or would ever be Kate's dog.

"He'd love this place. So much trouble to get into."

Kate smiled at the memories of the mischievous puppy Wally had been.

"What about Boyd? You think he's really in on this deal Kim talked about?"

Zane pulled his keys from his pocket. "That's a good question. I'm still waiting for the other shoe to drop. This all smells fishy."

Kate walked Zane to the front door. She wanted to leave with him, but she needed to learn to be alone in this house. "Dinner tonight? Bryce is coming."

"I've got work to do. And I'm working on finding next of kin for Lopez."

Kate stood on the porch as Zane stepped onto the garden path, headed to his car. "Maybe next week."

After Zane drove away, she walked out to her car and grabbed her work computer and paperwork. It may be her day off, but she had a murder on her hands. And if Boyd wasn't the killer, she needed to see who else might have killed Lopez.

Chapter 13

It had been a long night for Kim, and very little sleep. Jake awoke about an hour later, waited for her to roll off him, then he got out of bed. He needed to do his share of the household chores, and fix the steps leading to the dock. At Uncle Tucker's house, there was always a "honey do" list.

He kept checking his watch, making sure Kim didn't oversleep, because there were no second chances as far as Uncle Tucker was concerned.

Three o'clock. Jake moved the laundry from the washer to the dryer, then went to the bedroom to wake Kim. He gently nudged her. "Hey, sleepyhead, it's time to get ready for work."

Kim grunted and rolled away from him.

"Kim, get up. My uncle gave you a job, and I'm not going to take the wrath of Tucker if you're late."

She groaned and opened one eye. "I don't want a job."

Jake opened the curtains, even though the sun would make the room stifling hot. "Get up. I'm not your dad, and I'm not going to put up with a stubborn, spoiled brat. Either get up and take a shower or I'm calling a deputy to have you taken back to the jail. I'm not your get out of jail free card, Kim."

She slammed her hand down on top of the covers, then threw them back. "Fine. Go away. I'm getting up."

Jake left the room, vowing to give her only five minutes before calling the deputy's number. Two minutes later, when he heard the shower running, he breathed a sigh of relief. *So, this was what it was like raising a teenager,* he thought.

By the time she got to the car, she was more human than animal, and even smiled before she walked through the doors of Lucien's to start her new job. Jake said a little prayer, even though he didn't think it would be answered, that hopefully she was on her way to a new life.

Smiling as he drove back home, knowing his handyman work and chores were done, he looked forward to relaxing in a chair on the deck. Maybe he would even read a book. There wouldn't be many more nice days this season.

As he drove across the canal, his phone vibrated. It was Sergeant Gwilly. *Holy shit, isn't this my day off?*

"Where are you?" he asked.

"I'm headed home. Tucker gave Kim a job at the restaurant, and I just dropped her off."

"Good, we'll know where to find her." There was a

pregnant pause. "I need you to come to the house on M Street."

"You know I'm off duty, right?" That was the exact wrong thing to say.

"What the fuck did you just say?"

He tried not to whine as he said, "I'm on my way."

He hung up.

So, in police work, there wasn't such a thing as a day off, Jake thought as he flipped a U-turn in the middle of the street and headed back into town.

When he arrived at the house where he first saw Kim, he was surprised to see crime scene tape up and several police cars parked around the perimeter and in the driveway.

Heart jumping in his chest, he thought, *What the hell?*

An ambulance drove up before he got out of the car. Dreading what Gwilly was going to tell him, he walked up to the house.

"Underwood. Here. Now." Gwilly yelled from the side door of the house.

The front door had two-by-fours nailed over several pieces of plywood. They had busted that door up pretty good. When Jake looked into the side door, he knew shit had hit the fan. A dead man laid on the floor.

"Holy shit," was all he could say. "Holy shit."

"I'd like you to meet Kim's boyfriend, fiancé, whatever you want to call him, Andy Foss. He was alive and well last evening. That's when he posted bail and was released from jail. Don't be bothered by the fact that he doesn't stand up and shake hands."

From where Jake stood, Andy had been shot in the back of the head at close range, or so it seemed. CID was already on the scene, processing evidence.

"When did you get the call?"

"About an hour ago." He looked around the room. "Apparently a friend came by to visit, and when he saw Andy on the floor, he went next door and had the neighbor call the police."

Gwilly pointed to Jake's car.

"What?" He actually thought *what now?*

"Let's get some booties on, and I'll show you the rest of the crime scene. And I'd like to know where exactly your girlfriend was last night."

He really wished everyone would stop calling Kim his girlfriend. At least for now. He walked with Gwilly back to his car. His sergeant opened the trunk, then grabbed a couple pairs of shoe covers. He handed a pair to Jake. Just outside the house, he sat leaned against the wall and pulled the stretchy fabric over his feet. Jake did the same.

The side door led into the kitchen, which was where Andy Foss, aka Numb Nuts, lay in a pool of blood as the CID officers placed evidence numbers and took photographs. He only knew it was Numb Nuts because of the snake tattoo coiled around his right forearm.

Andy lay face down. Jake moved a little closer to verify he'd been shot in the back of the head at what looked to be very close range. He wasn't an expert, but he thought maybe the gun might have been pressed against Andy's skin.

"The bullet was found lodged in the cabinet door. Took out a few of the guy's front teeth on the way."

Jake looked around the other side of Andy to see his face. Burn marks marred his lips, and a bit of blood spilled from the side of his mouth. He couldn't see the broken teeth from where he stood. The officer held out his hand, showing Jake the bullet they recovered from the cabinet, then dropped it into an evidence bag. Pulling a pen from the breast pocket of his coveralls, he wrote the needed information on the bag.

"Whoever it was, Andy knew the killer. No forced entry, other than ours from the other night. And you can see that was nicely fixed up." Gwilly stepped aside so the CID officer taking photos could get a different angle.

A million things ran through Jake's head as he asked, "Did the neighbors hear anything?"

"Dornan's chatting with them now. He should be back soon." Gwilly rested the heel of his hand on his firearm. "There's another one upstairs."

Jake closed his eyes for a second, silently groaning, then followed Gwilly up the stairs he had climbed not so many hours ago.

In the same bedroom where Andy Foss had been tased and cuffed, a black guy lay flat on his back on the bed. Crimson spread out from under the body, turning a dark brown around the edges where it dried. This guy had been shot in the throat. He still had his hands wrapped around it, as if he'd tried to stop the flow of blood.

"Who's this guy?" He really didn't want to know.

"Leon Campbell. Ring a bell?"

He needed to sit down because the spinning in his head was making him nauseous. "Oh, shit. He was working with that cartel out of Mexico. What's the guy's name?"

"Oscar Silva. Goes by Payaso."

The officer who'd shown Jake the bullet said, "Clown? That's a little weird for a gang banger nickname."

"Payaso as in the movie *It*. Not the fun-loving clown at kids' parties. And he's more like a gang leader, not banger."

"All shithead bangers to me," the guy said and went back to his investigation, chuckling under his breath, "Payaso."

"Wow, this keeps getting messier and messier," Jake said.

"No shit. This is all wrapping up in a nice bundle now, isn't it?" The sarcasm heavy in Gwilly's voice.

"Time of death hasn't been established yet, right? I mean, we don't know for sure."

Gwilly grabbed Jake's shoulders and turned him around, then shoved him out of the room. "That junkie has some explaining to do."

"We don't know that for sure until we have a time of death established." *Why the hell was he defending her?*

"You're going to go pick her up, and bring her to the station."

"She's at work. It's part of her S.A.F.E. program rules. She needs to have a job."

"Good for her. But we need some answers." He quickened his pace as they descended the stairs.

"Can we see what other answers we get from the neighbors first? Tucker isn't into second chances, and if we snatch her away from work on her first night, and she turns out to be innocent, well…"

"Goddammit, Underwood. This is bullshit. You're not going to be a very good cop if you get personally involved in every incident you're a part of." They stood in the living room.

"It's not like that. I knew this girl when I was a kid…"

"That was a whole different world ago, Underwood. This is now. This just went from a drug bust to a double homicide. And what better opportunity to save your ass than to kill the assholes you just gave up? Only I think she killed them, then came to the station to offer up her information."

"I guess looking for the good in people isn't exactly a great quality in a cop." Head still spinning, Jake wanted to go outside and get fresh air.

"You'll learn that eighty percent of the time, we're dealing with the worst of the worst. If their lips are moving, they're lying. Didn't they teach you that at the academy?"

"Not in those exact words," Jake said.

"Outside." Apparently Gwilly read his mind. And as they walked back into the kitchen, he said, "You'll become jaded, and it won't take long. Pretty soon, you'll think everyone is lying to you. And they usually are. Right after they say, 'Okay, I ain't got no reason to lie to you, sir, this is the God's honest truth.'"

Once outside, Jake took a deep breath and closed his eyes for several seconds. He wanted to open them and have it all be a dream. Instead, he saw Dornan walking toward them.

"Hey, Sarge. I've got a little something to establish a timeline." He flipped open his notebook.

"Shoot."

"The lady next door said she heard a loud sound around one in the morning. But she didn't get up to see what it was because there was always something going on at this house. She said she thought it was fire-crackers or something."

Jake knew gunfire didn't really sound like firecrack-ers, but he kept his mouth shut.

Gwilly pulled out his own notepad and jotted down the time. He turned to Jake and asked, "What time did Kim come to the station?"

"I'm not sure. Tucker said he dropped her off, but he didn't say where." Jake thought about it. "I woke up and heard them talking somewhere around eleven, and then shortly afterward, Tucker and Kim left in his car."

To Dornan, Gwilly said, "Get the video footage from the exterior of the station. I want to know what time the Vega girl arrived at the station, and what her state of mind was. Maybe we can see it from the video."

"On it." Dornan turned on his heel and marched away like a good soldier.

"The D.A. is going to shit his pants when he hears about this." Gwilly handed Jake his cell phone. "And you're going to be the one to call him."

Jake hesitated before accepting the phone from him. "Don't you think he already knows?"

Gwilly pulled the phone back. "Never mind. I'll call him. And you're going to your uncle's place to keep an eye on Vega. I don't want her thinking she can skip out the back door on this."

Now even Jake doubted Kim's motives.

"I'll let you know what's going on, and I'll bring her back to the station as soon as I can."

"See if you can get Tucker to let her go early. We need to have a chat with this girl." The deep wrinkles around Gwilly's eyes, and his sour expression showed the stress this had caused.

Walking back to his car at a snail's pace, he dreaded stepping foot in Lucien's, only to find Kim had skipped out already. She was a player, and she'd played quite the hand so far.

On his way to the restaurant, a thought crossed his mind. Who was the friend who had found them? Jake picked up his phone to call Gwilly.

Chapter 14

Kate never left the farm. She hunkered down with her computer in the parlor, drinking sweet tea and surfing the 'net for information. Then she logged into the law enforcement database to check the names Kim had given them.

Geo Newton, Andy Foss, and Leon Campbell. She looked to see if any of them had been arrested together, and who their known cohorts were. The database held a lot of information, including tattoos. If she saw a guy with a bumblebee tattoo on his left wrist, and he'd been arrested, she could look the tattoo up in the database and find the guy's name, along with a photo of him, and close-ups of his tattoos.

Andy Foss had a snake on his arm. He'd been known to hang with Leon Campbell, and...Danny Boyd. Her fingers stiffened over the keyboard when she also saw her victim's name associated with Foss and

Boyd. Marco Lopez turned up in a lot of places, but the one that turned her stomach was the association with Oscar Silva, AKA Payaso.

Talk about a slippery sucker; Silva had never been arrested. But his name came up in several investigations involving drugs, or the lack thereof. Seemed any raid including Silva's name happened to come up with zilch. No drugs, no weapons. Kate knew this wasn't a coincidence.

Could Lopez have been working for Silva? From what she knew, Newton and Silva didn't much like each other. Drug territory wars and all. Seemed Silva might win that war, because he had the Sinaloa cartel behind him, or so the scuttlebutt implied. Why else would he be squeaky clean?

Azizi knocked on the door frame. "I didn't want you to be thinkin' I was sneaking."

Kate turned around to see the woman standing in the doorway, holding two large white ceramic bowls. "I'm sorry about earlier. You caught me off guard, and Victor hadn't mentioned anyone having access to the house other than the cleaning staff. And he said she came on Monday."

Azizi walked into the room and set the bowl on the table next to Kate's computer. "I hear you're a police officer."

Kate nodded, then looked at the bowl.

"Boudin. I cut it in slices and added it to red beans and rice. It's a little spicy."

"Spicy is good," Kate said. "Please sit. I'd like to get to know you better."

Azizi pulled up a chair. "I feel like I already know you."

Kate froze with the spoon halfway to her mouth. She put the spoon back in the bowl. "Oh?"

Chapter 15

If Kim was happy to see Jake, she sure didn't show it. She barely acknowledged him walking in the door. Uncle Tucker looked up and smiled wide.

"Jake, so good of you to come and help with the dishes for the dinner crowd."

Jake let out a faux laugh. "Right, dishes."

"You're not here to help out?" Tucker put his arm over Jake's shoulders. "It's a busy night. And your girl here, she's got experience, so she did okay for her first shift."

Jake looked back over his shoulder. Kim looked busy, but not happy.

"Can I ask you a question?"

Tucker looked at his watch, then looked around the crowded room. "Make it quick."

"Kim said her sister and her parents died in a car accident right in front of the restaurant. She said they were hit by a drunk driver. How come you never said anything about that?"

Tucker's brows almost disappeared into his hairline. "She told you that?"

"She said that's how she got hooked on opiates. Pain meds for her broken vertebrae. Then she started stealing her grandmother's pain meds."

"She stole her grandmother's pain meds all right, but that's not all she stole from the woman. And I don't know why she concocted that story, but her parents are alive and well. They moved out of town right after the accident."

"So they weren't killed by a drunk driver?"

"The drunk driver was Kim. Sixteen years old, and she killed a family of four. Only problem was she fled the scene, and by the time they found her, they couldn't prove she'd been drunk. Only reason she's not in prison is because she hid out for almost a day, claiming she blacked out and had no idea what happened."

Jake felt ill. Again, she lied to him. This was a doozy. He'd felt so bad for her, and almost understood how she'd become an addict. But she'd become an addict to forget she'd killed an entire family. She lived with that every day. But she deserved to live with it.

He had an obligation to take her back to the police station. His feelings for her had gone numb. She didn't care about him in any way. And to think he'd kissed her, and nearly had sex with her. Now, in his right mind, he realized he could end up with a sexually transmitted disease from her. He threw up a little in his mouth.

"I'm here to take her home a bit early." He cringed when Tucker squeezed his shoulders tight. "Sergeant Gwilly has some pertinent questions for her."

Tucker stopped squeezing. "More important than my dinner guests?"

Jake nodded.

"Not possible," Tucker winked.

"There's been a double homicide."

The words hung in the air.

"Not more important than my guests, because the dead guys aren't going anywhere, but I see the urgency." Color drained from his face. He got the implication.

"Kim isn't necessarily involved, but she knows the victims." Jake looked at the floor, embarrassed to ask outright. "Can she get off work early, so the D.A. and the police can talk to her? The sooner the better."

Tucker whispered in his ear, but it was loud because of the clatter of the restaurant at dinner rush. "This doesn't look good for your girl."

Jake grimaced. "I know, Uncle Tucker, I know."

When he looked back to the counter, Kim was gone. He panicked. Had she overheard the conversation and hightailed it out through the kitchen?

Relief flooded him as she came back through the swinging doors with an armful of plates.

Tucker looked at Kim, too. "Go. Take her. I'll take over the counter. But this better be worth it."

"I'm sorry, Uncle Tucker. I wouldn't do this if it wasn't crazy important."

Tucker walked over to Kim and asked for her apron and order tablet. Jake could see the puzzled look on her face. She looked at him and frowned.

Tucker said, "Go. Now."

Kim rushed over and asked, "What the hell?"

Jake grabbed her by the elbow to lead her out of the restaurant. No way was he going to make a scene in Lucien's.

"Wait, I need my bag," Kim said.

"I'll get it," Tucker said.

Tucker walked into the kitchen, then returned only moments later. He handed Jake the plastic grocery bag. "Thanks, Uncle Tucker."

Once out in the front of the restaurant, Jake said, "You look nice in that uniform."

It was a 1950s-style diner uniform in light blue with a white collar.

"Whatever. That's not why you dragged me out of there. Sure as hell not to compliment me." She yanked her elbow free.

"Let's get in my car." Only then did he realized he couldn't keep her from jumping out of the car while traveling down the road at fifty miles-per-hour. He debated waiting to explain the situation until they arrived at the station, or telling her right there.

"I'm not getting in the damn car until you tell me what's going on."

Jake glared at her, not liking her much at that

moment. "What time did my uncle drop you off at the police station last night?" Not that he expected the truth from her.

She frowned at him, then he saw a sort of recognition in her eyes. "He didn't drop me off at the police station. And I don't wear a watch, so I don't know what time it was. Though I do remember seeing it was before midnight on his dashboard clock." She kicked at a rock on the asphalt of the parking lot.

"Where did he take you?" He held his breath, waiting for the answer.

"He took me home, Jake, back to the house where I was arrested." She cocked her head defiantly.

"Is there something you forgot to tell the D.A. this morning?"

Now she looked everywhere but at Jake.

"Kim!"

All of her bravado faded in a heartbeat, and she began shaking like a naked woman in a snowstorm.

"I was scared." She collapsed in a heap on the asphalt.

Jake stood over her, not daring to get down to her level.

"I was terrified," she sobbed. "He was going to kill me. And he will kill me, if he finds out."

Jake braced himself for another bullshit story. "I swear to God, Kim, if you're lying to me, I'll kill you myself. And believe me, it will look like an overdose or an accident."

Not that he had any idea how to even administer an

overdose or where to get drugs, but he felt the words to his core. Pulling her up off the ground, he walked her to the car.

Opening the passenger door, he placed her in the seat. She sniffled and wiped her nose on the sleeve of her uniform. Uncle Tucker would be so pleased.

Once she was in the car, he went around to the driver's side, and prayed she didn't bolt in the time it took him to get inside. She didn't. She was too busy crying and shivering.

Jake grabbed a recorder from his duffle bag in the back seat. "I'm going to record this conversation, so don't say anything that you'll regret."

"Do I need a lawyer?" she whispered.

"I don't know. Do you?"

She shook her head and sucked in a deep breath.

Jake pressed record.

She sniffed up a nose full of snot, then said, "I went back to the house. All the lights were on, and I walked in the side door. Andy was sitting in the kitchen, smoking a cigarette, getting ready to shoot up. He'd already heated his rock to liquid and was pulling the syringe."

Jake could picture the scene: the filthy kitchen, the unsanitary needle, the burnt spoon.

"Anyway, he said there was enough for two, and I said I wasn't interested." She wrapped her arms around herself. "He flipped out."

"Did you use?"

She sat up straight, then looked at the recorder.

"No. No way. I promised Tucker I was on a new path. I wanted to, real bad, but I really just wanted to get my things and get the hell out of the house."

"What happened?"

"I lied to him. I told him I was tired, and I just wanted to sleep for a bit, then I'd shoot up with him when I woke up. It seemed to satisfy him, even though he said if I did it with him, I wouldn't be tired anymore. I told him I really needed sleep."

Jake stared at her, seeing a scared little girl telling her story. He had to remind himself of how convincing she was about the car accident to keep himself from pulling her close and comforting her.

"I went upstairs. But when I got to our bedroom, Leon was in the bed. I needed to pack without him waking up. I had a small bag packed and was ready to head out. That's when I heard voices downstairs. Only before I could go down and see who was there, I heard a gunshot. Then another. I panicked."

Jake hoped like hell she was telling the truth.

"Only seconds later, I heard someone stomping up the stairs." She looked at him, the terror in her eyes telling him she was not lying. "I opened the closet door and climbed into a box that I'd put in there a few weeks ago. I'd been planning to pack up some things, and so I had it in there for when I got around to it. I knew whoever it was would look in all of the rooms, and the closets, so if I just hid in there, he'd find me."

"How did you know it was a he?"

"The voices."

"Go on," Jake said.

"I crouched down, and pulled the box over my body. Right then, I heard another round of gunfire. Only this time it was in the same room I was in. I braced myself and waited for the closet door to open."

Jake held his breath, even though he knew the outcome.

"The door flew open, and I could hear him pushing the clothes around. I just knew I was dead. He was going to lift up that box, and I was dead as dirt." The tension in her shoulders released. "But he only kicked it. And I was smart enough not to get startled by it. Then he was gone."

Tears rolled down her cheeks and she sucked in a ragged breath.

"Who was he?"

"At first, I wasn't sure, because I didn't recognize his voice. But when he walked out of the bedroom, he said, 'That'll teach you assholes to try to rat me out.' And I knew it was Andy's supplier, Geo Newton."

Jake left the recorder running.

"Why didn't you tell my sergeant and the D.A. what really happened?"

"Right, you think they'd believe I had nothing to do with it?"

"Now they think you're guilty as hell, because you left out that part when you were begging for your deal. Did you forget to tell them that two of the drug deals were no longer going to happen because the players were fucking dead?" Jake shouted.

"If I left that out, they'd think I knew that Andy and Leon were dead. And I was in the house, so they'd think I did it."

Jake rolled his head back and rested it on the back of the seat. He couldn't even look at her. "Kim, you need to stop playing games. What you're doing is dangerous, and you're getting me involved. It's my day off, and here I am, looking at dead bodies, and tracking you down."

She turned her upper body toward him. "You saw them? Was it bad?"

Jake looked at her with wide eyes. "Are you kidding me? You were in the damned house, Kim, you saw them."

Her chin dropped to her chest. "I didn't. I waited until I heard a car drive away, and stayed where I was for another hour or so. Hell, I don't know how long it was, but I counted silently, so I wouldn't leave too soon. And when I did leave, I covered my face, and only looked forward, to get out as fast as I could. I was afraid of what I would do if I saw a dead person."

"Haven't you seen your share of dead people? Overdoses and all?"

"Never seen one up close."

"I have to take you to the police station. You'll have to tell them what you told me." He showed her the recorder. "You do have to go in and give a statement." He started the car.

"I can't go back there." She grabbed at his arm.

"Please don't take me back there. I'll never see the light of day again."

"Once they hear your story, I'm sure they'll let you go. Maybe they'll want to do a GSR test, but that's probably it." He pulled out of Lucien's parking lot and headed toward the police station.

"GSR?" She looked like a sad child.

"Gunshot residue. To see if you've fired a weapon."

A slight smile. "Oh, that's fine." Then serious. "If he sees me at the station, he's going to hunt me down and kill me, too."

"Who?"

"Geo. He's looking for me. I know it. I wasn't in the house, and he knows I was arrested, too. The only reason I gave him up was because I was afraid he'd come after me next."

"But you walked to the station from your house. Weren't you afraid he'd see you then?"

"I was in shock. I didn't even think about it. But later, his words rang in my head. Over and over. Maybe he thought I ratted him out, too."

"You did."

"But only because he killed my boyfriend and Leon," she defended.

"Why didn't you tell us about Geo this morning?"

"I don't know."

But she did know, and he didn't know how to pry it out of her.

"Can you please just take me home, and maybe

Darby or Gwilly can come to the house? Preferably without their cop cars?"

Jake looked at his watch. It was already after seven. The station was buzzing with this double murder, and she'd end up waiting in an interview room for hours. By the end of this, he figured he'd no longer have a badge, so he turned right on Highway 9 and headed back to the lake house.

Chapter 16

Much to Jake's surprise, Gwilly agreed to come to the house to talk to Kim. He said the turmoil at the police station was giving him a migraine, and he needed to get away. He also made it clear they'd be having a serious chat when this was finished, and Jake wouldn't have much of an ass left when it was done.

Relieved to not have to go back to the police station, Kim opened the grocery bag she had with her and changed from her uniform into a barely-there T-shirt and short shorts. Both were baby blue and clung to her body for dear life.

He didn't know how much more time they had together, or if this was the end. When Gwilly left this time, he could be taking Kim with him. Jake didn't believe a word the girl said at this point. He didn't even want her in his house, but he was stuck with her.

Kim pulled open the sliding glass door to the deck

and walked outside barefooted. She looked back and said, "Ready to at least enjoy the evening off of work?"

Jake felt that, as a cop, he never really was off duty, especially since she walked back into his life. He followed her outside and they walked down to the water's edge, sitting at the end of the dock. With their feet hanging over the water, not quite touching, Kim grabbed his hand and entwined her fingers.

"I like this," Jake said. "If only we were teenagers again, and we could have a do over, I'd have never left you."

Kim grinned. "I didn't realize how much I missed you until today. You were the only solid thing in my life, and then you were gone." She swung her feet back and forth, and he could barely see her as the sun set behind them.

"Who knew how much we'd end up needing each other?" He hadn't even considered her when he moved back to Peculiar, and yet he felt as if he'd been in love with her for years. He knew she was a liar and an addict, and yet the kid in him wanted her to be that innocent girl again. Even when he knew it couldn't be.

She laughed. "Oh, I don't think you really need me. You just need to fix something, and I'm here for the fixing."

In a way she was right, but he still thought he loved her. No way was he going to tell her that and scare her off. She'd already left him once, and Uncle Tucker helped her do it. He didn't know what he and Kim had,

Jake told himself, so he couldn't blame him. He could only fix what had been put in motion.

"Just tell Gwilly the truth, and tell the truth from here on out, and it's all going to get better."

She leaned against Jake's shoulder. "I have to tell the story all over again?"

"Just tell him what you told me. He's a good cop, and he's good at reading character." Jake leaned against her now, wondering, and hoping she'd tell the same story.

"I like this." She turned, stretched up and kissed Jake on the cheek.

Jake turned and kissed her on the lips. They were sweet and soft, and exactly as he imagined when they were kids sitting on the dock. It wasn't like the mad, passionate kissing earlier in the day. He felt the heat, sure, but he felt something else this time. Compassion. Love. Maybe she loved him, too. No, he couldn't go there yet.

Lying on the dock, with Kim on top of him, kissing, but still fully clothed, Jake saw headlights in the driveway.

Kim sprang up. "That's the cops."

He sat up. "Probably. Don't fret, I'll be here for you. Just like I said, tell him the truth."

When the headlights dimmed, Jake saw Gwilly walk around to the back door of the lake house. He must have seen them on the dock and called out. "Underwood?"

"Sergeant, we're headed back up to the house. Just

give us a sec." Jake leaned down and kissed Kim on the lips, then tucked his dick down in his pants, hoping Gwilly wouldn't see his erection, or what was left of it. "It's all going to work out just fine. I know it."

Jake could only see shadows on her face, but thought she smiled.

They walked back to the deck holding hands, but then Jake thought better of it and dropped her hand before Gwilly could see.

"Kim." Gwilly's demeanor standoffish. "Underwood. You want to talk out here?"

A string of white lights illuminated the deck, and it was late enough in the season that the mosquitos weren't hovering, so Jake sat in the Adirondack chair, and Kim and Gwilly sat at the picnic table. Jake lifted his hip and pulled the recorder from his pocket.

"Here." He tossed the recorder to Gwilly. "This has Kim's story. You can give a listen, so she doesn't have to go over it all again."

"Tell you what, Underwood, I've been doing this a long time. I'll handle this my way." He placed the recorder on the table. To Kim he said, "This shit has to stop."

Kim's good mood dropped off her face. "What shit?"

"The half-truths and lies. You came into the station this morning, begging for a plea deal, and offering up information in return. Then we find out the people you'd just ratted out couldn't care less that you snitched, because they're fucking dead."

Kim picked at her fingernails. "I was afraid if I told you about the murders, you'd think I did it. I was in the house, and my fingerprints were everywhere."

"Again, half-truths and lies. I want only the truth. If you can't do that, then we're done here." Gwilly stood.

Kim jumped up. "Wait. Look, I know I should have come clean, but I was scared. The only people who ever believed in me, or had my back, were dead. I was still in shock when I went to the police station. And I knew I had to give up something in order to stay out of jail. You don't understand, Geo has contacts on the inside and outside, and I was going to die before I ever got to trial."

Gwilly sat back down. "Geo Newton? Who does he have on the inside?"

She shook her head. "I don't know names, but I do know he's threatened us before. If we ratted him out for a lesser sentence, he said he'd know, and we'd be dead. Inside or outside, we'd be dead."

"You think maybe he was just blowing smoke up your ass to scare you?"

She continued picking at her fingernails, then put her right hand up to her mouth and chewed on the tips of her nails. Jake wanted to pull her hand out of her mouth. "Maybe."

"How are you feeling? Are you still clean, or did you shoot up last night when you went back to the house?"

She shivered and put her hand back on the table. "I didn't shoot up."

"Why do I even bother with you, Kim? You're your own worst enemy." He stood and pulled handcuffs from his belt. "Let's go."

Jake jumped up. "Wait," he said to Gwilly. To Kim, he said, "Remember what we talked about? Stop covering, lying, stepping around the truth. It's not going to work anymore. These people are smarter than you and your manipulation."

Kim looked as if he slapped her in the face.

"I snorted a line of meth." She dropped her head on the table and wrapped her arms over the back of her neck.

Jake wanted to strangle her with his bare hands. She told him and Tucker she wanted to change, and yet she went right back to that life and did drugs that night. Now he really knew she didn't want help.

"Was that so hard?" Gwilly said without feeling.

"But you're going to arrest me now," she said to the wood of the table.

"I'm not. If you keep telling me the truth, help us get Geo and whoever his supplier is, I'll keep my promise, and on Monday, I'll stand up with the D.A. and plead your case to the judge. But you can't do any more drugs, and you can't hold back."

"She has to take a piss test in the morning," Jake said.

Gwilly glared at him. "That's not a problem right now, unless you make it one."

She sat up straight, and told her story again. Only this time she added more detail.

"After I saw Andy in the kitchen, I knew I didn't have the strength to say no for long. I went upstairs and looked out the window in the hallway. I thought I saw someone creeping around the house." She looked at Jake.

"Did you recognize the person?" Gwilly took notes on his phone.

"I couldn't be sure who it was. But it was a guy. He wore all dark clothing and a hoodie. I couldn't see his face."

"How do you know it was a guy?" Gwilly asked.

Jake wanted to ask the same question, but bit his tongue.

"You know, guys move different from girls." She looked at Gwilly, then back at Jake. "He disappeared, and then I saw someone get into a car and sit for several minutes. Then the person started the car and drove away."

"What kind of car?"

"I'm not much into cars, so I can only tell you it had two doors, and it was a dark color. I tried to read the license plate, because I was sure it was one of Geo's men, but I couldn't see straight. I needed a fix kinda bad. The only reason I stayed at the window so long was because I was scared."

"Really scared, or drug induced paranoia?" Gwilly stared at her.

"A little of both maybe?" She said it as a question more than a statement.

"What next?"

She picked absently at her skin. "I had to pee, so I went into the bathroom. Leon, or someone, had left a meth baggie on the counter, and I took the blade out of the razor in the medicine cabinet and scraped the edges of the baggie, trying to salvage the dust. Then I snorted it. The relief was overwhelming. But the amount was so minimal, I knew the high wouldn't last long."

"How long were you home when you saw the man and the car?"

"I don't know. Like I told Jake, I don't wear a watch. Maybe an hour." She wrapped her bony fingers around her wrist and rubbed.

"You said you saw Leon upstairs in bed, and soon after you heard the gunshots."

"I think so." She rubbed hard at her wrist. "I mean, yes, that's how it happened. I wanted to pack a bag just in case, you know?"

"In case of what? Were you preparing to run?" Gwilly stopped tapping in notes with his stylus, and looked at her.

Jake looked at her. His instincts were right; she was going to run.

"Andy said we might need to move quickly." Her leg bounced. "I told him I didn't want to run. And he got pissed at me."

She'd failed to share this detail with Jake. After everything, all of the promises, she was going back to Andy, back to the gutter.

"That's when he told me we needed to save ourselves. Narc out Geo, and then once the cops cut us loose, we'd blow this shitty little town." She gave a weak smile.

Nothing she told him was the whole truth. Or was she embellishing for Gwilly? How was he supposed to know? He could have kicked himself for his stupidity.

"Even though you had a court date on Monday, you were going to run?" Gwilly's voice went low.

"No, we were going to ask for a deal on Monday. That's how I got the idea to come in and talk to Officer Darby." She grinned with her teeth showing this time, like she was offering a morsel. "Andy and Leon were dead. I didn't have any other friends. I didn't know what to do."

Her words stabbed at Jake's heart. Didn't she think he was her friend? Hell, no, he was just convenient. This wasn't the same Kim he'd known as a kid. He had to stop fooling himself.

"Kim, you need better friends. Andy and Leon were going to get you killed. Not only that, they both laid the entire drug operation at your feet. Said you were Geo's girlfriend, and that you were there that night because you were setting up the next major shipment."

Kim froze.

Jake couldn't keep quiet. "Well, Kim?"

She turned swiftly to look at him. "What the hell? No. I mean…"

"Why do you think Leon and Andy were out of jail when you went to the house?"

"I didn't think to ask. I mean, I was out, wasn't I?" She looked like a deer in the headlights.

"And you think you weren't being watched? You think, after all of the work I've done, I was just going to let the system turn you loose?"

"Was it your guy who I saw sneaking around the house?" She was visibly shaking now.

Jake cursed himself. Why hadn't they told him they'd been watching Kim and the house? Why would they tell him? He should have suspected they wouldn't just let her walk away.

Gwilly looked at Jake. "Still think your bitch can be saved?"

Jake wanted to leap out of the chair and beat the shit out of his boss. Instead, he gripped the armrests of the chair until the wood dug into his skin. He didn't answer.

"So, who were you fucking, Kim? Andy or Geo? Or both?" Gwilly asked, not really caring.

"Fuck you," she responded without much energy.

Chapter 17

"Let's start again. And this time you can tell me the story, knowing that I know the truth." Gwilly relaxed his posture to a friendlier position.

"Fine, Geo and I were lovers, but only because he gave me drugs for free. And he gave me money to keep an eye on his operations." She gripped the picnic bench as if it were a lifeline. "But I wanted out. I even told Andy I wanted out. I think that's what Andy told Geo last night that got him killed."

"I thought you said Geo was mad because he thought they ratted him out?"

"That, too. It's such a mess. And when Geo found me in the closet, he made me promise to go to the cops and tell them all about the drug deal going down. Tell it like Andy and Leon were still alive. He trusted that I'd do it for him. And he said the only reason I wasn't dead was because he needed me to buy him some time."

Feeling the bile rise in his throat, Jake wanted to

wrap his fingers around Kim's throat and choke the life out of her. She'd played him hard.

"You know your story doesn't really add up?"

"Like I said, I was high. It's all sort of a jumble. I just know that Geo killed Andy and Leon, and he told me to walk to the police station and tell them I wanted to plead 'no contest' to the charges, and ask about the S.A.F.E. program to show that I was sincere. Then I was to tell you and the D.A. about a couple of drug deals going down next week. They were deals he knew about, and he figured it'd be at least that long before you found the bodies. Who the hell knew someone would call the cops so soon?"

"So why are you ratting out Geo now?" Jake asked. The fire in his words burning his throat.

She looked at Jake, her eyes melting into tears. "Because I want out. I did everything everyone asked me to do, and nothing went as planned. Geo said he'd come and get me Monday, after the judge granted me into the program, and we'd be gone. Either way, with Andy or with Geo, I was outta here."

"So, let's say we hadn't found the bodies right away. What would have happened when we arrived at the location of the drug buy?" Gwilly's words friendlier now, coaxing.

"Geo set up one of his rivals. You'd have walked in on a drug buy. A fucking huge deal going down at the warehouse. His rival would be gone, and he'd lay low for a while, then we'd be back in business." She wiped her tears away with the back of her forearm.

"I thought you were blowing this town?"

"That's what he promised, but then I realized he'd never leave. Not unless the cops got too close. He didn't want to start all over in a new place, learn the ways of the cops, and build a new clientele. That's when I knew I was on my own. My life is over as I know it. And when Tucker offered me a job, I gladly took it. If I get into the S.A.F.E program, I'm going to work it like my life depends on it, because it does."

The contradictions in her statements were overwhelming. Jake wasn't even sure she knew what the truth was.

"You'd be required to participate in a twelve-step program, too. You need new friends, and I don't think Jake can do this by himself." Gwilly grabbed the recorder from the table and put it in his pocket. Then he pulled out a brown evidence bag, unfolded it, and put it on the table. "Jake, I need the shirt she was wearing last night when she left the house. I want to do a GSR test on it."

Jake tried to remember what she was wearing. So much had happened that night, and his mind was a jumble.

"It was your shirt, Jake. I had on the shirt and sweat pants you gave me."

No, it wasn't. She'd changed back into her own clothes. Her lie jogged his memory. He didn't think the shirt was still in the house. Without responding, Jake went into his bedroom and dug through her duffel bag. He found the clothes she'd put in the washer and put them in the evidence bag. He wasn't going to say anything, but then he didn't want to stoop to her level. He'd already stooped low enough.

When Jake handed the bag to Gwilly, he said, "She had actually changed clothes. She and my uncle were sitting at the kitchen table, and I remember she had changed back into the clothes she'd been wearing when she got out of jail. She'd washed them. Later, she put them back on when she thought I was asleep."

Kim looked at Jake as if he were the devil.

"I'm not lying for you, Kim, not when I know the truth. That's not how relationships and friendships work."

He saw the will blow out of her with one breath. "Fine, you're right." She looked at Gwilly. "My mistake. Not a lie, just a mistake."

Gwilly stood. "Stand up," he said to Kim.

Kim looked at Jake, then at Gwilly. "Why?"

"Kim, nothing you told the D.A. is true. There's no drug deal going down. You readily admitted to doing meth while you were at the house. Stand up and turn around."

Jake didn't even have time to blink before Kim bolted.

He leapt forward and reached out, catching the end of her ponytail, wrenching her back.

"Motherfucker," she screamed.

"Shut the fuck up," Jake said. He helped her off the grass, never letting go of her ponytail.

Gwilly stepped up. "Kim, you're under arrest…"

Chapter 18

Bryce Trident loved his job, especially when he worked with Dr. Ogelsby. But Ogelsby was gone, and he had to train a new forensic pathologist to his ways. Yes, he would train this new doctor. Dr. O had taught him well, but he'd also been a student of Bryce's. Bryce learned to train doctors when he was in graduate school for nursing. He got tired of being pushed around and unappreciated, so he started his own school, in his mind, and it didn't take long before the doctors called for him specifically.

"What do you see here?" Dr. Glen McClaren, his new student, asked.

"I see a dead body."

"Cut the crap, Bryce, tell me."

Bryce had looked the body over before Dr. McC came in. In fact, he'd prepared the body for the young doctor. And by young, Bryce thought he was in his early forties. Dr. O had been nine-hundred years old, plus or minus a decade.

"Based on the toxicology reports, and the weird bruising at the top of his head, I think this guy either died, or would have died of a drug overdose, had someone not pulled him to a standing position by the hair on the top of his head, and shot him through the base of his skull."

Dr. McClaren frowned, looked closer at the top of the victim's skull, then said, "That very well could be. I agree with the assessment of the overdose. This guy was dead one way or the other. The bullet made a point somehow. Made it final, just in case the drugs didn't."

Bryce knew his job well. He'd been prepping and examining victims for more than a decade. More often than not, the victim proved to be a drain on society. Yes, innocent people died too, and he had a harder time with those bodies. After his first year in the forensic lab, he chose to see the bodies as peanut shells. The soul could still hover, but it no longer resided inside the peanut shell. He had no issues tearing apart a peanut shell. And the best part of the job: no attitude, well, except from a few cops and the doctor. He didn't have enough time with the cops to get them trained, but Dr. McC was coming along nicely.

"We have three people from Peculiar: two shot in the back of the head, and one in the throat, but we don't have the bullet from the first victim."

"Have we gotten the tests on the bullets?" Bryce asked.

"They pulled one from the cabinet of the house where this guy was found. That went in for testing. I haven't had a good look, but the throat shot may have lodged in the victim's spine. No bullet was found in the room where he was killed. Once we have it, I'll have the lab test it. I'm a betting man, and I'd bet at least these two bullets are from the same gun."

Bryce snickered. "Duh."

"Smartass. There's always a chance it's different guns."

"Do you think the guy found in the trunk met the same gun?"

Dr. McClaren shrugged. "The burn pattern certainly looks similar on him and on this patient. But I doubt they'll ever find that bullet."

A knock sounded at the door to the lab. Bryce turned to see Kate's face smashed against the small window.

"That's my sister. She's working this case. Can she come in?" Bryce said.

Dr. McClaren concentrated on Andy's scalp, but nodded.

Bryce waved Kate in.

"Thanks. Who do we have here?" Kate said as she came through the door and immediately went to the closet to cover and glove up.

"This is Dr. Glen McClaren," Bryce said.

Kate pulled on the gown, not bothering to tie it, then slipped gloves over her hands. She already had her hair pulled back, so she covered it with a surgical cap.

"Dr. McClaren is the victim? I thought you were working on one of my victims."

The doctor looked up. "We aren't really set up for visitors. Is there something I can help you with?"

Kate blanched. She'd been in the lab many times with Dr. Ogelsby. "Oh, hi, I'm sorry. I didn't know we had a new forensic pathologist."

"Dr. O retired. You should really try to listen when I talk to you, if you're going to keep visiting unannounced," Bryce said, then handed Dr. McClaren some forceps.

"Dr. Oglesby trained you well," Dr. McClaren said.

"Yeah," Bryce said, trying hard to keep the sarcasm from his voice.

"We're looking at poor Mr. Andy Foss," Dr. McClaren said. "And you are?"

"I'm looking at you, looking at Andy Foss," Kate said.

"He meant, who are you, stupid." Bryce rolled his eyes.

Kate glared at Bryce. "I'm Kate Darby. Andy Foss might be part of another murder I'm investigating."

Dr. McClaren stood tall and turned to look at Kate. He pulled down his face mask and smiled his broad smile of pearly whites, the crow's feet in the corners of his eyes deepening. Bryce could see Kate appreciated the man's military haircut, broad smile, dark brown eyes, and tanned skin. Bryce didn't really think of Dr. McClaren as good-looking, until he saw him through Kate's eyes.

Bryce worked hard to be handsome. Several laser treatments for the acne scars he'd gained as a teen made his skin smoother, but he'd never have that polished skin most guys had. He still had huge pores and had learned to live with them. The drug binge he continued until deciding to get a life didn't help, either. It had taken its toll on his body. Being vain, Bryce worked out religiously, when he wasn't working. He showered at least twice a day to keep his skin fresh, always worried the acne would return. He'd never have the dark skin women loved, but he didn't care. Women still slept with him, and that's all that mattered. He wasn't looking for Mrs. Right, only Ms. Right Now. He didn't have time for a relationship. He spent too much time with work and keeping his appearance maintained.

"Nice to meet you, Miss Kate. Bryce tells me you're his sister. You don't look anything alike. I guess that's lucky for you. But you sure act like siblings."

Bryce flipped the doctor off behind his back.

"We're foster siblings. We were both adopted by the same family," Kate said, moving closer to the examination table.

"Different last names?"

Bryce cleared his throat. "I was older when I was adopted, so I kept my last name. My parents were cool with it. A man needs to keep his family tree thriving. If I took their name, my tree would die with me. Can't be having that."

The doctor returned his concentration to Andy. "Absolutely not."

"Not like he'll ever stick with a girl long enough to have kids, but maybe a one-night stand will get pregnant," Kate said.

"If I learned one thing from my foster dad, it was," Bryce changed his voice, "'always wear a raincoat, never trust the girl.'"

"Funny thing, Dad told me to never trust the guy," Kate laughed.

Once the doctor turned away, Kate wiggled her brows. Bryce stuck his gloved finger in his mouth to gag. He pulled it out just as the doctor looked up.

"What do we know?" Kate stepped up to the table.

"We know he's dead," Bryce said.

"You're in a mood. Didn't get laid last night?" Kate said.

"Definitely siblings," Dr. McClaren said, laughing. "I'm pretty sure the fentanyl killed him. From the looks of it, he was either dead, or nearly dead, from the drugs, and then someone lifted him by the hair on the top of his head to put the bullet through the back of his brain. Knocked out a few teeth in the process. Point blank range. We're going to compare the burns along with the bullets. Whoever did this didn't realize how close to dead our Andy already was, or he wouldn't have wasted a bullet." He shrugged, then said, "Or maybe he still would have."

"Interesting," Kate tried to sound interested, but Bryce knew better.

"What are you looking at now, Dr. McClaren?" Kate asked.

"Please, call me Glen," he said, pushing Andy's shoulder off the table and turning him on his side in preparation to roll him over. "Look here."

Bryce helped reposition Andy onto his stomach and flat on the table.

"Hesitation, I think. Look at that," Bryce said, pointing to the bullet wound at the base of Andy's skull.

"Good call, Bryce. This isn't a solid burn mark. It's like the gun was held against him, but then moved before they pulled the trigger. This guy's brain stem was obliterated by the bullet." He looked at Kate. "Forgive the lack of medical terms; I find cops usually haven't studied medicine, so it's easier to speak in laymen's terms."

"Thanks," Kate said.

"Would a person who'd killed before hesitate?"

"I'm not a killer, but I'd think unless this guy was a friend or relative, a person in his line of work wouldn't hesitate. But I can't be sure."

"Our current person of interest for this killing isn't a novice. I can't be sure he's killed before, but I damn sure don't think he'd hesitate. If this goes the way I think it will, this guy was killed by the dealer he worked with. Those guys don't have feelings for the people who screw them over."

"Maybe it's something for your notes," Glen said.

"What about the other body at the scene?" Kate asked.

Bryce was sure she didn't remember the victim's name without the file in front of her. "You mean Leon?"

Kate nodded, not humble enough to be embarrassed she didn't remember the name.

"I haven't looked at the toxicology report yet, and we haven't examined the body. Either way, they are both dead." Dr. McClaren continued to poke and prod at the top of Andy's head. He looked up at Bryce. "Grab the saw and let's give this guy a skull cap."

With that, Kate said, "I'd better get out of your way. Thanks."

"For what? We didn't tell you anything," Bryce said, handing the skull saw to the doctor.

"For letting me know about the fentanyl and the burn marks. The fentanyl tells me some bad drugs are obviously being circulated. I'll have to talk to Zane about this."

Dr. McClaren said, "Zane?"

Bryce answered before Kate could. "Her ex-husband and her boss, Sergeant Zane Gwilly. Hopefully soon to be Lieutenant Gwilly."

"Not married, huh?" was not the response Bryce expected out of the doctor.

"Not married," Kate said. "You?"

McClaren answered with a smile Kate didn't see. Bryce smiled because he knew this guy was hot for his sister. "Not anymore."

Bryce didn't want to be a witness to their flirting, so

he said, "Got time for lunch? We're taking a break right after Andy."

"I don't. But come by the house after work. You need to decide which room you're going to live in."

Bryce shook his head. "I'm fine where I am. That place is too far from the hospital."

"The other day you were hot to move in. You said the bedrooms were larger than your apartment. Have you been talking to Zane? He said the house was too far from town."

"I haven't been talking to Zane. I still need to think it over. I'm not good with change," Bryce said.

"What place?" McClaren asked.

"My sister inherited a pecan farm from the grandfather she never knew."

"That's sounds interesting. You'll have to tell me the story sometime," McClaren said as he started the skull saw.

Kate didn't hear him as she stripped off her hat, gloves, and gown before bolting out of the room.

Bryce laughed out loud. "I'll see you tonight. Want me to bring pizza or something?"

Kate was already out of the room and didn't respond. He'd text her later.

Chapter 19

Kate hadn't taken a real day off since she found the body in the trunk of the Mercedes. Though she'd spent more time at the plantation house, which she really needed to find a new name for, than she did at her place. She liked the open air of the property. And even with the stifling hot summer temperatures, a breeze always seemed to blow. She never thought of herself as a country girl, but she could change that.

She hadn't seen Azizi in a day or so, and looked over at the tenant house as she got in her vehicle. She'd wanted to stop by and knock on the door, just to see the inside of the building, which looked like an old, square log cabin that had been plastered over in spots. She couldn't see in the windows, and doubted the place even had electricity.

Kate reversed out of the driveway and as she stopped for possible traffic on the road, she thought she saw someone standing on the porch of Azizi's house.

She'd seen them in her rearview mirror, but when she looked again, no one was there. Her imagination, she supposed.

And then Glen's bright smile popped into her head. He couldn't be much older than her, and he seemed nice. She wondered if he might be single. He seemed interested enough when she said she wasn't married. If the doctor hadn't been cutting into the skull to expose brains, she might have invited him to visit her new home. Or would she?

It had been a long time since she shared her bed with a man. The few hook ups with Zane didn't count, since she left his house before Zane could roll over and fall asleep. She still loved him so much it hurt, but she couldn't hurt him by trying to repair the past and move forward. She wasn't that kind of person. She'd already torn his heart to shreds when she divorced him. And no matter what she said, he couldn't understand that the fault didn't lie with anyone other than her total inability to commit. And she'd tried, Lord, she'd tried, but somehow being alone was her station in life.

Kate's phone buzzed and she looked at the screen. Yes, cops had to text and drive. Hell, they typed on their laptop and drove. She hated the distraction, but it happened to be part of her job.

The text from Zane read, *Video here*.

A smile broadened across Kate's face as she pressed the accelerator harder. Finally, maybe a break in the case. Though the people who died weren't fine, upstanding citizens, and possibly the world wouldn't miss them, they were someone's son, father, brother, and she needed to deal the cards of justice, no matter who they were. Criminal or not, she promised she'd treat every case as if the victim were Mother Teresa, deserving of justice.

Parking her car, Kate jogged up to the station entrance and swiped her ID. Looking down the hall, she saw Zane. "Hey, are you set up already?"

Zane, who'd been walking away from her, turned. "I have us in interview one. Grab a cup of coffee and join me."

Her rotation had her on days this week. Usually she dreaded the day shift because of the boredom and the stupid calls she had to go out on, not to mention the brass. Not this week. She planned to work her case along with working the streets. She could investigate better during business hours when managers worked and stores were open.

She didn't see a coffee cup in Zane's hand, so when she stopped at the coffee machine, she pulled two paper cups from the stack, slipped a sleeve over both, then poured creamer in before adding the coffee. Carefully placing lids on both, she listened and felt for the final pop that let her know the seal was tight. Spilling hot coffee on her hands wasn't how she wanted to start her day.

One cup in each hand, she walked to the interview room. She placed one cup in the crook of her elbow, balancing it against her ribs as she opened the door with her now free hand. As soon as she got the door open, she used her booted foot as a doorstop and grabbed the coffee cup. Hitting the door with her hip, she walked into the room.

"I'm all set up," Zane said. "Hope you're wide awake. There's a lot of video to go through."

Kate handed Zane a cup. "I wasn't sure if you'd had any yet this morning."

Zane gladly accepted her offer. "I wanted to get set up. This was my next task. Thanks."

Kate set her cup on the round Formica covered table. "Should I grab a notebook?"

"I've got two here." Zane reached down into the case by his left leg and handed Kate a spiral pad. "We'll need to mark down the name or number of the tape, and the time stamps of places we're interested in."

Kate sat down and pulled a pen from her breast pocket. "Can't we just take our own video of the video?"

"We could, but we can't use that as evidence if we need to. It could be manipulated. And we'll need to mark the video to make it easier should this go to court. They don't want to wade through all the video again just to find what we already found."

"Great. Sounds like fun," Kate said, and meant it.

"It's going to be tedious, so be prepared."

"Awesome. But I'd like to get this done and get out there. I don't want the captain thinking I'm slacking." Kate opened her notepad and scribbled circles at the top of the page to get the ink flowing in her pen.

"Slacking would be to not investigate these murders to our full potential."

Kate settled in as Zane inserted the first of a stack of discs into the player. He picked up the remote control, and she rolled her eyes. How hard could it be to just stop and start from the player that was on the table and within a few inches from either of them?

An hour and a half later, Kate appreciated the remote, as Zane played, fast-forwarded, paused, rewound, and played again, at least a hundred times. "Want me to take over before you get carpel tunnel?" she asked.

"I'm good. The problem is that we don't know when the car arrived in the parking lot. It's only when we see the car that we'll have any idea where to start. We can play the video at double speed until we spot the Mercedes."

Four hours, five cups of coffee, and two bathroom breaks later, Kate swore off coffee. And when they settled back down, she said, "Stop, go back and then play in slow motion."

"How far back?" Zane asked.

"I don't know, maybe ten seconds?" Kate leaned closer to the screen, her eyes tired and dry.

Zane did as he was told, the clock on the video read, 12:15:30 when he hit play and slow motion. They had started each video at 22:00 and it had been slow going.

"See that?" Kate pointed at the screen.

"What are you looking at?" Zane, irritated, leaned closer to the screen, too.

"It's the Mercedes. At the McDonald's drive-thru."

"I wonder if they have video cameras in the drive thru," Zane said.

The car drove away from the pickup window, stopped at the curb, then turned left. Out of sight. "Damn."

"I didn't see any McDonald's trash in the car. Not even a spare french fry."

"The car had been thoroughly cleaned, though. Maybe that was Marco driving," Kate said.

They had watched video footage from six different cameras by the time they saw the white Mercedes at McDonald's.

As Zane put the seventh disc in the player, he said, "At least now we only have to watch from midnight. Not all day."

"We haven't been watching all day as it is. Lord, shoot me now if we have to go back and watch these again. I thought for sure starting at ten o'clock would be good." Kate sighed at the thought of being able to skip umpteen hours of footage. There were twenty-seven cameras in the Kroger parking lot. They had a long way to go.

Slouching down in the seat, Kate craved coffee, but she didn't want to get up and lose more time. Besides, coffee led to peeing, and peeing took more time than making coffee. It was the damn vest. But she wasn't about to get undressed to take it off, only to have to get dressed again to go out on patrol.

Barely paying attention, she found her thoughts straying, when they both saw it at the same time.

"There," Zane said, just as Kate sat up in her chair.

"Boom," Kate punched her fist into the air and sat up straighter. "Slow it down."

In one-quarter time, they watched.

The white Mercedes pulled into view of the security camera at 2:12 am.

"That's not the same car that was at the McDonald's," Kate said.

Zane leaned in, as if getting closer to the screen would tell him more. "What makes you say that?"

"The license plate color. I know it was too far away to read, but the plate on the car in the drive-thru was colored. This one is Texas white with black." Kate pointed to the back plate as the Mercedes rolled out of view.

"What the hell? I should have known that was too easy," Zane said.

"Be patient, Grasshopper."

The car circled around and came to a stop in the second to the last parking spot in the row. Kroger was only open until midnight, and at that time of night, the lot was nearly empty. They waited as the car continued to idle. Or so it seemed, since the brake lights continued to shine bright. Then the car seemed to move a little, and Kate saw the reverse lights flash as the driver must have put the car in park. No more brake lights.

Impatient, Kate wanted to speed up the video to full speed, but then she didn't want to miss anything and have to rewind, only to lose more time. She already had the time jotted on her notepad, and tried to scribble more notes without taking her gaze from the screen.

"What's he doing?" Zane asked.

"I'd bet fifty bucks he's wiping down the inside of the car," Kate said.

"I'd bet dinner, but not fifty bucks," Zane said.

Kate ignored his response.

A few minutes later the driver's side door opened. A wiry looking person with loose fitting jeans and a light-colored hoodie got out. He didn't look up or look around. Pulling the hood further over his head, he tightened the strings, then shut the car door with the sleeve of the sweatshirt over his hand. It was impossible to see if it was male or female, but Kate assumed male because of the clothing. He shoved his hands in the pockets of his hoodie as he walked away.

"You see that?" Zane said.

"What, his white sneakers?"

"Sneakers? Does anyone call them sneakers anymore?" Zane laughed.

"Shut up, who cares? See what?" Kate leaned back away from Zane.

"The limp." He rewound the video, then replayed in regular time.

And there it was, slight, but definitely limping on his left leg.

"And he doesn't even come close to resembling Boyd, does he?" Kate said.

"No one said Boyd dropped the car, just that he stole it."

By the time they saw the guy drop the car in the Kroger parking lot, Kate's eyes burned from staring at the screen for hours, barely blinking. She looked at Zane, who rubbed his eyes.

"Let's take a break. Grab lunch or something. I have a headache," Zane said.

"My eyes are killing me. Let's grab something from a drive-thru and stop at CVS for eye drops and Tylenol."

Just as they stood, the door opened. Chief Rambone walked in. "Hey, how's it going? Find anything?"

Chapter 20

After wasting ten minutes updating the chief, they finally left to grab lunch. Kate couldn't wait to get back and go through the rest of the video to see Boyd's part in this crime.

Drive-thru it was, and they each held their own bags, ordering from Sonic because they knew it would be quickish, and Kate loved their pretzels.

Zane tore open his bag from the side and used it as a placemat on the table. He dumped his onion rings on a napkin, then unwrapped his slinger. He had ordered three slingers and two orders of onion rings, along with the largest pickle juice slushy they offered.

Kate ordered the bacon slinger, tater tots, and a diet Sprite. She pulled her food from the bag, smashed the bag down, and placed her items on top, then reached for the remote to turn on the video.

"Your fingers aren't greasy, are they?" Zane asked as he stuffed an onion ring in his mouth.

"I haven't even eaten anything yet, and I'm saving my pretzel for dessert." She clicked the remote to start the video.

They watched the same camera video, now that they knew which one they needed, in double time while they ate. Both had decided during their drive to get food that Boyd had to have jacked the car right before Kate tried to pull him over. Or at least within the hour, but they wanted to look through the timeline from two to five just to be sure nothing else happened in the interim.

They'd finished their meals and put the garbage in the trash receptacle in the kitchen before getting to the next juicy part of the video. The time stamp: 5:23 a.m.

Boyd entered the scene from the lower right side, just walking around the parking lot like he didn't have a care in the world. Because you know, it's perfectly natural to be cruising the Kroger parking lot on foot at five-thirty in the morning. He wove between cars, as if looking for something specific. He stopped to look in the passenger side of a red Pontiac Grand Am, tried the door handle (locked), looked around to see if anyone was looking, then walked down another row of the parking lot. Stopping at a newer Ford 250 Super Cab, he looked in the driver's window, then went around to the passenger side. Kate realized he could see if keys had been left in the ignition from the passenger side, but not the driver's side. That little prick was actually actively looking to jack a car.

Then Boyd looked up. It appeared he spotted the Mercedes parked eight spots out in the next row. He looked around, then walked directly to the Mercedes. His modus operandi with this car changed from the others. Constantly looking around as he walked to the car, he didn't look around the car or check the passenger side. Walking straight up to the driver's door, he reached for the handle and opened it.

Zane paused the video. "Did you see what I just saw?"

"He wasn't smart enough to make it look random. His movements at the Mercedes were completely different from the other cars. He knew that car would be there, and that the keys would be in it."

"Just making sure we saw the same thing." He turned the video back on.

Boyd immediately started the car and drove away.

"Someone told him to jack that car," Zane said.

"Why else would he be randomly walking around the Kroger parking lot at five in the morning? They don't even open until six. But I'll bet employees were there at that time."

Zane took a long sip of his pickle juice slushy, face puckering like he'd bitten into a lemon. "I think it's time we had another chat with little Danny Boy."

Kate cringed. "Is it bad that he makes my skin crawl?"

Zane laughed. "It would be bad if he didn't."

"He's still in the county jail, isn't he?" Kate asked.

"As far as I know. I heard he couldn't post bail. But who knows? I'll check into it and get him transported back here."

"No, I need to get out of here. And we can work patrol on the way. Let's go to the jail and pay him a visit there." Kate stood, grabbing her garbage to toss it in the trash, but made sure she pulled her pretzel out first. She took a big bite then asked, "Are you coming with me?"

"Damn, this investigation is getting me so far behind on everything, including paperwork." Zane stood, pulled the lid off his drink and tipped the cup up as he leaned his head back.

Kate could feel her taste buds pucker as she watched him finish off the slushy. "I don't know how you drink those. It's just gross."

Zane chucked the cup into the waste bin. "I love them. And it's probably only going to be around for the summer, so I'm getting as many as I can before they quit selling them. Let me stop in and talk to the chief. I'll meet you at the jail." Zane opened the door, holding it for Kate.

Kate walked down the hall toward the parking lot, and Zane went in the opposite direction. As she walked out the double doors, the stifling wet heat took her breath away. Every day she worked, she wore four layers of clothing, so any time she heard someone bitch about the heat, she had the urge to throat punch them. Good thing being a cop made her think twice before doing stupid things.

"Hey, how's your murder investigation?"

Kate looked up to see Jake walking toward her. She fought to keep from rolling her eyes. "It's going. How's your girlfriend?" She just couldn't help herself.

"Very funny. I'm sure I'm the laughingstock of the department over Kim."

"Not really, it's even too stupid for anyone to talk about." Kate felt especially salty toward Jake for some reason.

"Not nice at all," Jake said, his normally jovial face drawn.

"Look, you're young, and you let your dick do the thinking for you. It's a guy thing. Girls are idiots, too. Look how many corrections officers fall for the loser inmates."

Jake's brows furrowed. "Really?"

"You're nothing special, sorry to have to tell you. But like I said from the beginning, rein little Jakey in, and keep your mind in the right place. Besides, how gross to have sex with a junkie like that. Who knows what she's taking in just to get a fix?"

Jake turned a shade of green.

Kate smacked him on the arm. "Please tell me you didn't have sex with that girl. Please!"

"I've gotta go. This conversation isn't appropriate for work." He stormed by her and into the building.

Kate laughed hard as she walked to her car. "He's gonna need a thicker layer of skin."

"Hey, wait up," Zane called from behind Kate.

"I thought we were meeting at the jail?"

"Change of plans. Let's take my car."

Kate walked to the passenger side of Zane's vehicle. "What's with the change of heart?"

Zane unlocked the passenger side as he climbed in the driver's side. As Kate climbed in, she looked at Zane, to see if something may have gone wrong in his talk with the chief, but she didn't dare ask.

Zane's movements seemed jerky and rough, so Kate waited him out. Once on the road, he said, "Something about the raid the other night has been bugging me."

"Are you going to tell me what it is?" Kate watched their surroundings as Zane drove.

"Did you find any drugs on that Kim chick the night of the raid?"

"No, nothing upstairs. Just an empty baggie on her. Enough to arrest her, that's all."

"Right? Only the one guy trying to get rid of a little bit of weed."

Kate stopped scanning the streets and turned to look at Zane. "That house was a notorious drug house."

"But Boyd did have those baggies up is butt cheeks," Zane said.

"He was outside the house, and no way did he have time to take his pants down and shove that shit up his ass crack."

"You never know, but I think they were tipped off," Zane said.

"It didn't even dawn on me. But now you say it, there should have been enough drugs in that house for distribution." Kate mentally smacked herself for not seeing it earlier.

"The problem is everyone and their partner knew about the warrant. If we have a leak, it'd be impossible to find at this point."

Kate thought about the process and timeline leading up to them busting in the door of the house on M Street. Zane was right; they made no secret about the warrant, or the raid.

The scene from the house played in Kate's mind: the chaos, everyone running in different directions, the guy upstairs fighting with Dornan, her little Angry Betty who turned out to be Underwood's childhood heartthrob. Most importantly, the suspect in the kitchen, getting rid of just a little bit of marijuana. Barely enough for a misdemeanor. Something about the situation stunk, and it wasn't the skunk weed.

"Anyone we arrested a CI?" Kate asked.

"Good question," Zane said. "I'll have to look into it. The biggest thing is the murders. Foss and Campbell don't seem smart enough for much more than local small time. You know?"

"But you know how it is, if their lips are movin', they're lyin'."

"Ain't that just about everyone we deal with?" Zane snorted in disgust. "I wanted to be a cop to help people. Never in my life did I think my perspective of people would change so drastically. I actually think everyone is lying until proven otherwise, even good people."

"Thanks," Kate said, knowing she fell into the people he spoke of.

Zane's disgust with people in general, and always expecting lies, hadn't helped their relationship. Kate had grown up not being trusted, so she had issues with people not believing her. Sure, she told her share of lies, but for some reason, Zane never believed her when she told him she'd never done drugs, never been arrested for drug use or dealing. Of all the issues, too many one-night-stands, black out drunk, rebellious, she'd done it all, but never drugs. When she found out he tried to get her juvenile records, she flipped out. That was the beginning of the end. She already second guessed herself for committing to a relationship that terrified her, and him looking into her past behind her back destroyed her trust.

Growing up in the foster system, trust meant every-thing to her. She couldn't say she never lied, but she tried to be upfront, even when caught having sex with more than one guy at a time. If her mom taught her anything, the lies catch up to you. She didn't have the energy to keep it all straight when she was a kid, and had even less energy now.

"Not everyone is a liar, Zane."

"We don't need to go there again," he said. "Espe-cially not now. I don't want to go into the jail with tension between us."

"Whatever," Kate snapped.

"No, not whatever, Kate. Drop it."

"Fuck you." Kate leaned against the passenger door and looked straight ahead.

The crackling of the radio and dispatch were the only sounds in the car for the rest of the drive.

Chapter 21

The light at Market and Hawthorn turned green, and just as Zane started forward, a silver Kia flew through the light doing at least fifty in a thirty-five zone.

"Oh, hell, no," he said, flipping on his lights and siren. He keyed his mic. "117 headquarters, copy signal 18 HQ."

"Go ahead, 117."

Zane described the Kia and their location, then said, "Stand by for stop, HQ."

"Standing by."

"Don't we need to get to the jail?" Kate asked, anxious to talk to Boyd.

"We aren't in any hurry." Zane floored it and burned rubber as he turned left from the middle lane. As he turned onto Market, most of the traffic parted ways.

"Heading west on Market Street," Zane updated over the radio. He blared his horn for a car who somehow didn't see or hear them coming up, and the car promptly ignored them. "Get that license plate and run it," he said to Kate.

Kate did as she was told, writing down the plate number and make and model of the car. Nothing pissed her off more than assholes who didn't give the right of way to law enforcement or first responders.

The Kia, still going fifty in what was now a forty mile per hour zone, cruised through a yellow light this time. Zane slowed for the intersection, not wanting to be t-boned for rushing through and having someone hit them, then floored it. They followed behind the Kia for about four-hundred feet before the driver finally looked up and slowed.

"Holy shit, that idiot was on his phone," Kate said.

"Could you tell if he was texting or talking?" Zane asked.

"Does it matter?" Kate asked. "He had his phone in his hand."

The entire state of Texas now had a hands-free law, but Peculiar had implemented the law in 2015 and saw phone related accidents decrease since.

The driver practically dropped the phone as he slowed and pulled over into the right lane before coming to a complete stop.

"117 HQ, stop is at Market and Mulberry. Occupied by one. Stand by."

"Standing by."

Kate and Zane exited the car at the same time, Zane approaching from the driver's side, touching the left rear fender above the lights. Kate did the same on the passenger side, holding her hand on her service weapon as they approached.

She could only hear Zane's part of the conversation, but that didn't matter, her focus was on the movements of the driver, who was alone in the car. She pushed the button on the mic at her shoulder. "229 HQ, silver Kia occupied by one."

"10-4 229."

"Do you know why I pulled you over?" Zane asked.

Kate tried to hear the response.

"Not exactly, but yes, you were going fifty in a thirty-five zone. But speeding is the least of your problems. I need your license, registration and insurance, please."

The driver turned out to be female, but had her hair pulled back at the nape of her neck. She did look a little masculine, but not enough to think she was a dude. Kate felt bad for assuming it was a guy. Then again, it was a Kia, she should have assumed it was a chick, because this little boxy Kia was a chick car for sure.

She continued to search her car's center console, seeming to scramble and get frustrated.

"Ma'am, do you have your license at least?" Zane asked.

Kate noticed she didn't go into her purse first like most women would if looking for a driver's license. Unless she kept her ID in her phone case, which wasn't unheard of.

Kate didn't hear the response again, but she heard the tone of the woman change.

"Okay, just give me your name, Social Security number and date of birth." Zane pulled his notepad from his pocket.

Kate listened.

"Okay, I'll need you to get out of the car," Zane said, his tone no longer friendly, but stern.

Kate heard an emphatic "No!" from the driver.

She walked around the back of the car, ready to assist Zane.

"Ma'am, I asked you nicely to get out of the car. You haven't shown me any identification or registration."

"I know my rights, I'm not getting out of the car." This girl who looked to be in her early twenties spat the words.

"You've apparently been misinformed of your rights, ma'am. He's asked you nicely to exit the vehicle. I'm now asking, please exit the vehicle. If I have to ask you one more time, it won't be asking. I'll remove you from the car."

The girl's head snapped toward Kate. "I know my rights."

After giving the girl a few more minutes to calm down and comply, Zane reached for the door handle to open the door. Locked. He reached inside to unlock the door, and the girl moved to roll her window up.

Kate pulled her taser. "Stop right now. Roll that back down, or I'll tase you. RIGHT NOW!"

Kate nearly screamed the last two words, which stunned the girl more than looking at the prongs of the taser. She rolled the window back down.

Zane unlocked and opened the door, and Kate reached in, grabbed the girl by the arm and pulled her from the car.

"Ouch! Get your hands off me. You can't…"

Kate said, "You tell me one more time how to do my job, and I'll demonstrate exactly all the things I can do. You've refused to provide identification, you've disobeyed a lawful order, and you're being disruptive. This could have been a simple traffic stop, for which you'd have gotten a ticket for speeding, running a red light, and using your phone while driving, but now it's much, much more."

Kate had the girl's hands cuffed behind her back before the girl realized it. Once she realized her position, she fought the cuffs.

"You're gonna have some nasty bruises if you don't cut that out. They aren't made of fur."

The girl stopped fighting the cuffs and slammed herself against her car. "Aren't you going to search me?"

Kate turned the girl to face her. "You're full of attitude, aren't you? You do realize you're making this worse by the second."

"I'm going to reach into your handbag and look for a wallet or your driver's license," Zane said as soon as the girl stood still.

"No, you're not! You don't have permission to enter my car and get my purse."

"Then tell me your name, Social Security number, and birthdate."

Fifteen minutes later, they had the information they needed. Ellie Otterman had a long list of traffic violations, which now included driving on a suspended license.

"You realize you have a warrant?" Zane asked after running her information through their system.

"Whatever," was all she said.

Kate read Ellie her rights, then patted her down. "You're not hiding anything on your person, are you? Like drugs in your butt crack? Because if they find drugs on you at the jail, you're also going to have a felony charge."

Ellie looked over her shoulder. "Why don't you just check for yourself?"

"Well then, let's get you in the car. We were headed to the jail, anyway."

Zane said, "Save the jailer a trip to pick you up from our holding cell."

Once in the car, Ellie cried and cried, apologizing for being a bitch, making promises in return for them dropping the charges.

Zane and Kate didn't speak to her or each other. Then they transferred her to the custody of Holt County Jail.

"That was fun," Zane said.

"You call that fun? I get so sick of the disregard for

authority. I always start off giving them the benefit of the doubt, but it seems the person behind the wheel doesn't feel the same."

"No weapons in the car. We're alive and well to complain about it. I call that fun."

Kate laughed.

After jumping through hoops as if they were just your average everyday visitors to the jail, which included turning in their weapons to the front desk, Kate and Zane were escorted to a private room in the jail.

"I feel like we should be able to keep our weapons," Kate said.

"We aren't the authority here; the sheriff's department is. And it's safer to not have a weapon handy. Too easy to pull it and shoot the asshole in the head." Zane wasn't kidding. At least, his tone sounded dead serious.

"Sorry about the liar thing in the car." Kate hated to succumb to Zane's attitude. But she had told him to fuck off, and she felt bad about that. Sort of.

"It's always the same old thing with you, over and over, Kate. Nothing changes. I'm not sure you understand that at work I'm your boss. And you don't tell your boss to fuck off. If I wasn't in love with you, you'd have been written up enough times to have lost your job. You need to figure out the boundaries. I let it go when we were married. But we aren't married anymore."

She wanted to take back her apology, but she literally bit her tongue to keep from saying anything. If she'd had her phone on her, she'd have pulled it from her pocket and pointedly ignored him. The words stung, because he spoke the truth. She'd become so accustomed to being married to him and fighting, that she no longer distinguished between married fighting and being insubordinate with her boss. She'd never talk back to the captain or chief like she did to Zane. But she'd never had killer sex with either of those men, either. She threw up a little in her mouth at the thought of having sex with Chief Rambone.

A jailer led Danny Boyd into the room and adjusted his cuffs so he could be shackled to the table, which had been bolted to the floor. Kate thought Boyd looked cute in his pink pants and yellow and white striped "Property of Holt County Jail" top. Boyd didn't look up until the jailer had him secured.

"Oh, shit. What do you want?" He leaned back, scooting his chair as far back as he could.

"We're here to talk to you about the murder of Marco Lopez." Zane leaned forward, resting both elbows on the table, his forearms crossed.

Kate had no desire to lean forward. Her skin already crawled from being in Boyd's presence. She'd play good cop if Zane let her.

"Ya'll don't listen. I got nothing to do with no Meskins. Ain't my scene."

"You may not have killed Marco, but you're not innocent by any means," Kate said.

Boyd lowered his head and swayed it back and

forth, as if listening to a song only he heard. "No, no, no. You don't get it. I din't kill that dude. Marco is into some scary shit, and I ain't into that. I don't want to die or nothin'."

"Look, Danny, cut the shit. We have video of you jacking the car from the Kroger parking lot. You're not innocent on many counts, but you're sure as shit guilty of grand theft auto."

He shook his head again. Kate wondered if he might have a slight mental disability. It looked like he tried to process what was being said, but it got jumbled.

"It's not stealing when someone tells you to pick up the car, is it?" He looked at Kate, his eyes pleading.

Just as they'd suspected. Boyd knew that car was there. Kate tapped her toes a little, doing a "we were right" happy dance in private.

Zane cleared his throat. "So, you're saying Marco told you to come get his car from the Kroger parking lot at five in the morning?"

Boyd grimaced. "Well, not exactly. Like I said, I ain't in business with that Meskin. But it don't matter, cuz Marco's dead. He can't press charges. You got the car back. And I ain't gotta prove I was told to pick the car up. Popo gots to do their job."

"Popo?" Kate nearly choked on the word.

"Y'all know, the po-lice. Popo," Danny said, as if schooling a two-year old.

Zane rolled his eyes.

"Who told you the car would be in the parking lot,

Danny?" Kate did lean forward now, wanting to grab Boyd by the throat.

"I didn't say no one told me the car'd be there," Danny whined.

"You just said exactly that," Kate said.

"No I din't. I just saw the car. Maybe I recognized it. Was gonna move it closer to the front door and all."

Kate couldn't even muster a chuckle at Boyd's stupidity.

"Let's start from the beginning, Danny. Why were you walking around the Kroger parking lot at five in the morning?" Zane said.

Danny scooted his chair forward a little. His arms getting tired, Kate was sure of it. Then he shrugged. "Couldn't sleep, so I went for a walk."

Zane looked down at his notepad and flipped through a few pages. "You live on the other side of town. Why wouldn't you go for a walk closer to home?"

Danny stammered, then started again. "I was hangin' with friends, you know? They passed out and I was wide awake, so I went for a walk."

"Okay, what's the address of your friend's house?" Zane asked.

Danny said, "What's the address?"

A typical stalling technique when someone doesn't have an answer, they repeat the question.

"That's what I asked. What's the address of the house where you were hanging out with friends?" Zane said the words slowly.

"Well, it wasn't a house. Was an apartment, you know?"

"And the address?" Zane asked patiently.

"I don't know. I didn't drive there. Marc...Manny did."

Kate caught the slip up. So blatant.

Zane pretended not to hear it. Because there's no way he missed it, Kate thought.

"Okay, your friend Manny drove you there. What's the name of the apartments?"

Danny shrugged, having no idea he'd messed up. He truly thought they didn't catch his mistake.

"Okay, let me ask you this, who came by to talk to Marco?"

"What you talkin' crazy for? Marco wasn't there. Sheeit, that's crazy talk." Danny looked down at his fingers, which he drummed on the table.

"Danny, you said his name, now just fess up, or you'll be an accessory after the fact, and you're going to prison for murder," Kate said.

"Murder? No, man, I thought we were past that. I ain't murdered no one." Danny stopped drumming his fingers and tried to reach up and move the hair from his forehead. He winced when his bony wrists met the resistance of the metal cuffs. "Fuck."

"So, once again, from the beginning. You were at some apartments near Kroger. You couldn't sleep, so you went for a walk. You saw Marco's car. How long before that did Marco leave the apartment you were at?"

Chapter 22

Jake knocked on the open door to Chief Rambone's office. "Sir, the captain said you wanted to talk to me?"

Rambone looked up from the paperwork on his desk. He pushed it aside and said, "Yes, please have a seat." He flicked his hand indicating the seat next to his desk.

Jake looked at the seat across from his desk and really wanted to sit there. Sitting next to the desk at the side made Jake feel like he'd gotten in trouble in elementary school. But he sat there, because who was he to argue? "Is everything okay?"

"As far as I know it is," Rambone said. "I wanted to talk to you about Kim Vega."

Jake felt the heat rise from his core and flush his neck and face. "Oh, Kim, what about her?" He almost choked on the words.

The very mention of her name made his insides

squirm. He'd made so many mistakes the week he rode with Corporal Darby. He thought it was all behind him, especially since Kim remained in jail, but now this.

"I hear you two had a past."

Jake nodded.

"She stayed at your house for a few days?"

The office smelled like stale tobacco, and Jake wondered if the chief had a nasty habit. Not that he had anything against chewing tobacco. Heck, they were in East Texas after all. He figured more people chewed than smoked tobacco. Or maybe not. But the smell wasn't smoking tobacco. He knew that smell. With his dad being a jockey, he swore every other jockey, along with his dad, smoked. Something to keep them occupied so they didn't eat. And in that profession, they obsessed about weight as much as any supermodel. He knew he was deflecting by thinking of other things. Thank goodness he heard the chief's question before he had to ask it again.

"No, sir, she just stayed the one night. The first night was when she went back home, then arrived here at the station the next morning."

"Okay, I see. You two still close?" Rambone picked up a pen and wiggled it between his middle and forefinger.

"We were friends when I was like twelve or so. I hadn't seen her in years. I guess I felt bad things had gone so wrong for her since I saw her last. But goodness, she's changed. And she prefers lies to the truth."

"Bless her heart," Rambone drew out the words.

"Anyway, she won't be an issue for me. I learned my lesson. From here out, I'm steering clear of that girl. And I'm going to remind myself, using Kim as an example, not to let it get personal."

"Well, that's harder than you'd think. But I'm not worried about it. You'll make plenty of mistakes in this job. As long as you're doing your best and don't get anyone fired, hurt, or killed, it's usually something we can move on from." Rambone took a deep breath. "I'm wondering what Kim may have told you."

"Told me? Like what?" Jake leaned forward, now curious as to what Chief Rambone wanted.

"Did she say anything about the night of the raid? Like if they knew the cops were coming? Anything about being tipped off?" He'd gone from wiggling the pen to tapping it on the desk, sliding it through his fingers, then flipping to the other end, tapping and repeating the movement.

Trying to stay focused on the conversation, and not the pen, Jake said, "I don't recall anything significant."

Rambone slapped the pen down on the desk. "Think, son. Did she mention any names? We're just wondering why almost no drugs were found at the house, when we know they were dealing large quantities from that location."

"She didn't mention anything about the raid directly, or that she knew about it. And almost everything she said, she'd turn it around and have another story two hours later. I didn't know what to believe." He wasn't sure what else to tell the chief to make him happy. He didn't know anything else. "Like I said, I learned my lesson. I've wiped my hands clean of that girl."

Rambone frowned, then picked at something in his teeth. "Don't walk away just yet. We may need you to get close to her. I need you to get her to trust you, in case we need more information."

"Honestly, I don't know what is the truth and what's not with Kim. So I'm not sure what good I'd be." This wasn't what Jake expected at all when Rambone brought up Kim's name. And he wasn't sure he liked where this was heading.

"She knows something she's not saying. For right now, don't ask any questions, just go visit her when you have time off. Let her know you're on her side, even if you are a cop."

Jake cringed. He wanted nothing to do with Kim, and now he was being told to visit her in jail. "I don't think that's a good idea, sir."

Rambone slammed his hand down on the desk, and the pen he'd been playing with bounced off the edge, falling on the floor. "I'm the one who decides what is and what isn't a good idea. And I think Kim needs to think she has a friend. Obviously, no one has come to bail her out this time, so she's been abandoned for the moment. You can be her savior."

Jake opened his mouth to speak, but Rambone held his hand up.

"Be gone. I've got a lot on my plate today. Just make the time to visit that girl."

As Jake walked down the hall to find the captain, he wondered what had happened to the person who bailed Kim out the first time. And was even more curious as to who it was.

Chapter 23

Boyd used the too long fingernails on his right hand to dig under the too long fingernails of his left hand, removing the dirt and grease, then he wiped the grime on the sleeve of his shirt. Kate half expected him to lean down and remove it from his finger with his mouth.

"What time did Lopez leave the apartment, Boyd?" Zane asked again.

Switching to clean the fingernails on his right hand, Boyd said, "I didn't say that Meskin was at the apartment, man."

"You didn't have to. Just tell us what happened. Like Sergeant Gwilly said, start at the beginning. Like when you arrived at the apartment, who was there?" Kate worked hard to keep the edge out of her voice.

Boyd concentrated on his fingernails for a full minute before responding. "What am I gettin' for talking to you?"

"I haven't talked to the D.A. yet, but I'll see what I can do," Zane said.

"I ain't talkin' till I have a deal, you know? I need a good deal," Boyd whined.

Zane stood. "Fine, I'll go see what I can do, but by the time I do that and come back, I won't need your information anymore. Good luck in here."

Kate followed Zane's lead, put her pad of paper in her pocket and stood. She didn't bother to address Boyd, just followed Zane to the door.

Boyd tried to stand, but got caught up by his hand-cuffs. "What do you mean, too late? You ain't got nothin' or you wouldn't be here talking to me."

"That's where you're wrong. We have someone in the other room, who also has a story to tell. The first one to talk will likely get the deal from the D.A. Not that I can promise what the deal will be, but maybe they'll drop the grand larceny charges."

"I didn't larceny anything. Fuck. I got that shitty fucking lawyer. I shouldn't even be in here." Boyd sat back down and dropped his head down to his hands.

Kate wasn't sure, but she thought Boyd might be crying. She looked at Zane, waiting him out to see what happened next. This was her case, but he was her boss, so she bit her lip and waited.

Zane turned around. "You crying, Boyd?"

Boyd wiped his face on his sleeve, in the same place he wiped the dirt from his fingernails, then looked up. "No, I ain't a crybaby. But you gotta help me. I don't belong in here."

"You talk, and if I think you have anything to offer, I'll talk to the D.A. and maybe see about getting you another attorney." Zane walked back to the table, pulled out the chair and sat.

Kate hesitated, not sure if Zane meant to stay and listen, or if it was a gesture. When he didn't make a move to get right back up, she pulled out the chair next to him and sat.

"Start talking," Zane said.

Boyd wiped his eyes one more time. "Okay, Marco was there. But he got a call and left. I don't wear a watch, but it was at least a few hours before I went for my walk. I might have heard him say both Newton's name and Payaso's."

Kate looked at Zane, who raised his brows so high, deep wrinkles showed on his forehead.

"What about them?" Zane asked.

Before Boyd could answer, Kate asked, "Who has the limp?"

Boyd perked up. He knew that answer. "Payaso. He got shot in the shin a few years ago. I think he can walk fine, but wants everyone to remember what a badass he is."

Kate thought it probably was a real limp, since no one was around when he walked away from Marco's car, and was still limping. Or maybe it had become habit. She could still see the video in her mind of the guy in the jeans and hoodie walking away.

"Did Marco say anything before he left the apartment?" Zane asked.

"Nothin'. But he looked pissed." Boyd sniffed and rubbed his nose. "Marco don't usually mess around in Peculiar. He's got his own territory. I don't know much else about him, but he had some good shit he was passing around that night. Said he got a new supplier."

"What shit was he passing around? Heroin? Meth?" Kate asked.

Boyd laughed. "No, man, Marco's all about the ganja."

"What about Payaso?" Kate knew he pushed heroin, since he'd moved on from meth.

"What about him?" Boyd asked.

"What's he selling?"

Boyd shrugged.

"Don't start that shit, Boyd. You haven't given me enough to get me to talk to the D.A. yet. Keep those lips flappin' and I'll tell you when you're getting close."

Kate stifled a laugh at "lips flappin'".

"Was Newton at the apartment?" Zane asked.

"Naw, man, I ain't seen Newton around. Shit went down with him and Payaso, and Newton sorta went underground." Boyd rolled his head around on his neck as if he was just getting warmed up.

He never sat still, Kate noticed. Always moving his hands, body, and feet, like on a meth high. But he'd been in jail long enough to have come down off any high.

"What about his girlfriend, Kim?" Kate asked.

Zane shot her a glare. What? Was she not supposed to ask any questions?

"That's the bitch you got's willing to talk. Good luck with that. Unless you're offering her a fix, you ain't getting nothing. Dumb cu—" Boyd looked at Kate, then swallowed the word, "bitch. And she ain't Newton's chick. No way. I only seen Newton with hot chicks. Don't think he hangs with addicts. Prolly doesn't even do drugs himself. Always seems too put together. I ain't never seen him high."

"So, Geo Newton and Kim Vega aren't a couple?" Zane didn't sound like he believed Boyd.

Boyd seemed to be pondering his answer. "Unless that's the falling out with him and Payaso. But like I said, Kim ain't classy enough for Newton. You think Lopez drove a nice car, Newton gots a Range Rover, man. He ain't letting a skank like Kim in that thing."

"Who did the drugs in the M Street house belong to?" Zane asked.

"Weren't no drugs in that house. They all been moved." Boyd sat back in his chair now, smug.

"Yeah, there weren't any the night of the raid, but if there were, who would they have belonged to?" Kate said.

"If I was a bettin' man, I'd say Payaso. Maybe. Or coulda been from Newton. Again, the bad blood coulda been a territory thing." He shifted in his seat and looked at the door. "So what's Kim told you?"

"We're talking to her next," Zane said. "And if she gives us more information than you do, she's gonna walk, and you're gonna sit in here and rot."

"I ain't no player. They don't tell me nothing. I just

do my job, which is delivery." Boyd realized too late he'd implicated himself. "I mean, I deliver food to the house, like I'm GrubHub or something."

Kate coughed. "Kim's already offered up information on the murders of Leon and Andy."

She could actually see Boyd stop breathing. She waited. For the first time, Boyd wasn't moving. Not even the wheels in his pea-sized brain seemed to be turning. She waited for him to finally take a breath or pass out.

Green in the face, Boyd said, "Leon is dead? Andy too? Oh shit, there might be a turf war going down."

"You didn't know?" Zane asked.

"Last time I seen Leon and Andy, they'd posted bail. I ain't heard nothing since." He took a deep breath to replenish the oxygen to his brain. "Does Kim know?"

"She does. Like I said, she's already given us information," Zane said.

"But you said you ain't talked to her, so how?" Boyd looked terrified.

"It came up in conversation when she was at her friend's house," Kate offered.

Boyd leaned forward, hands gripping the edge of the table. "Bet she didn't tell you she was fucking Andy, did she? I'm telling you, she'd blow anyone for a fix. But last I heard she was Payaso's girl. Then I saw her with Andy the night of the raid. Like, her face in his lap kind of with him!"

Kate's mind went back to the forensic pathologist's words. It looked like Foss had been lifted by his hair and shot through the back of the head. But he'd already been pretty much dead from the overdose. She knew the notes were in Zane's hands by now, because Bryce had brought over a bottle of wine that night and said he'd typed up Glen's notes and emailed them to Zane and the chief. Kate had been pissed off that Bryce hadn't sent a copy to her, when he produced a hard copy of his notes, along with crusty French bread and tomato basil olive oil. They drank wine, ate bread dipped in olive oil, and Kate finally talked Bryce into moving in with her at the house. When he left, she went to bed with the report and read it over and over.

"You're saying Kim was really Payaso's girl, but the night of the raid she was with Andy?" Zane asked, even though he knew the answer.

"Wow, that bitch got Andy killed." He shook his head. "But why kill Leon? I liked Leon."

"You didn't like Andy?" Kate asked.

The look on Boyd's face spoke volumes.

Zane pulled his phone from his pocket. He grimaced and put it back. "I'm not sure you gave us much. But I'll see about getting you a new attorney, anyway. Not sure how much it will help you. You did commit a crime against another person, and you know we don't usually drop charges for that sort of thing, unless you're giving us hard evidence of a crime."

"Is it a crime to hide drugs when you know your crib is going to be raided?"

"Nope. The real crime is in the fact that someone

was warned, and I'm pretty sure you can't give me a name there," Zane said.

Boyd looked at the floor. "But we knew. Leon got a call. They cleared out the house only an hour before you bashed in the door."

Zane stood. "And that's another issue we'll deal with."

"What if I could find out how they knew? Would that help me?" Boyd asked.

"It might. But for now, I need to talk to Kim."

Boyd jumped up. "But I told you everything I know. And I told the truth, the whole truth, and nothing but the truth, man. I should get the deal, not her."

Kate and Zane walked out together as Boyd continued to scream about how he'd been wronged.

Chapter 24

Kate liked the chief well enough, but didn't like meetings in his office. He made her feel like a little girl being reprimanded, even when she wasn't in trouble. But she knew they needed this sit down. Zane said he could do it, but she wanted the promotion, not him. His was pretty much guaranteed.

Rambone's door stood open, so Kate knocked and walked in without being invited. She knew if she waited, he'd want her to sit in the chair at the end of his desk, and that felt weird to her, so she helped herself to the chair on the other side from the chief. Somehow, having the full desk between them felt better.

"Did you hear about the forensics on the murders of Foss and Campbell?" she asked as she sat.

"I did. I sent a text message to Gwilly," the chief said.

"Oh, he didn't say you sent the text." Now she felt stupid. "He wanted me to talk to you about what's going on with the M Street murders, but apparently you already have all the information."

"I don't know about that. Let me hear it from your perspective." He leaned back and crossed his arms, which did nothing to make Kate more comfortable.

Kate looked at her notes, which she brought in with her, because she didn't want to miss anything that might later come back to haunt her. She told him all about Kim and what Zane had gleaned from her when he arrested her at Jake's house, then about Boyd, and about her visit to the morgue. She ended with the revelation Boyd had said about them being tipped off, and that he somehow thought Kim may be the reason for Foss' death.

"But it's the text that has me puzzled. Why would Foss be killed with one gun, and Campbell with another?" she said.

"The hesitation marks you mentioned, they give me pause. Not something you'd see from a hardened criminal like Payaso or even Newton, though I do think Newton is more of a pussy than people think he is."

Kate smiled at his choice of words for Newton. She didn't know Newton from the system, just to see his face or hear his name. She hadn't had any run-ins with him. But she knew him to be tall, and his mugshot showed bright red hair cut in a short afro, and pale skin. She might have called him handsome if she didn't know all about him.

"I don't know, but Boyd seemed to think he was a pretty boy, with his Range Rover and pretty girlfriends.

Said a guy like Newton wouldn't have anything to do with a girl like Kim Vega."

Kate noticed Rambone's arms tightened. "I'm not so sure. Newton paid the bail for Vega."

Kate's brows raised. "That I did not know."

"It's something you should have known. Maybe they were hooking up. Maybe he got pissed off when he heard about her and Foss."

"That girl, Foss, Payaso, and now Newton. I don't even know what to think."

"And don't forget the number she did on Underwood."

Kate smirked.

A uniform cop knocked on the door. "Excuse me, Kate, this just came for you. I thought you might want it."

Kate stood and accepted the envelope. "Thanks, Booger."

She tore open the envelope before sitting back down. Reading, her eyes went wide. "Well, well, maybe we have a suspect after all." She handed the paper to Rambone. "Kim's clothing tested positive for GSR."

Rambone tapped his fingers on the paper. "Interesting." He looked up. "What is your next move?"

"I guess I go have a talk with Kim. She seems to know more than anyone, if we can get her to tell the truth." Kate turned to leave. "She's too low on the food chain to have been the person who knew about the raid. Once we find out who the drugs belonged to, then we know who got tipped off."

"I'm not sure I get your logic," Rambone said.

"That house was a dealer house, but no one in that shithole had the money or smarts to be running the operation. They were the middle man, buying from a bigger fish. If the bigger fish was Newton, then he was somehow tipped off, and he let them know. If the drugs belonged to Payaso, then he was tipped off. Lopez could have been our guy, but he was dead before Zane had the warrant, if I remember correctly."

"Okay, and finding that person may also tell us who killed Lopez," Rambone stood, as if he planned to follow Kate out of the office. Instead, he held the door, nearly pushing her out of the office. "Connect Newton or Payaso to the killing of Lopez. That's the best explanation. They all seemed to be on the same level, and all seemed to be stepping on each other's toes." He closed the door behind her.

Kate stood outside Rambone's office, contemplating her next move. Then her stomach growled and she knew her next move was to get food.

Kate sat in the parking lot of the convenience store, munching on a Butterfinger and drinking coffee. Her cell phone rang. She looked at the caller ID, but didn't recognize the number. With all the robocalls these days, even a local cell phone number wasn't really a person calling. Kate recognized the area code, and the prefix looked like a cell, but she let it go to voicemail. Plenty of times she answered, and it was a robocall, which was fine, because she didn't care about hanging up on a recorded voice. Especially the one telling her that her

Social Security number had been flagged and it was going to be suspended, or some such nonsense. Once she even pressed the number they said to press, and let the person on the other end know she was a cop. She asked for the real phone number of the company this man worked for, and somehow the line disconnected.

She looked down. A voicemail. Robocalls rarely left a voicemail. She picked up her phone, swiping and tapping to get to the call.

"Hi, Officer Darby, my name is Geo Newton. I really need to talk to you. Please call me back."

Kate's heart skipped a beat in her chest. How had he gotten her phone number? She thought back to anyone who might have it. Should she call him back?

Curiosity got the better of her. She hit redial.

"This is Corporal Kate Darby. Did you just call me?" She tried to sound pleasant, but knew she failed.

"Look, I know I shouldn't be calling your private phone, but I need to talk to someone. My name is Geo Newton."

"How did you get my phone number?" Kate didn't care about the rest until she knew how her privacy had been compromised.

"Look, I don't want to say, okay? Someone you know gave it to me, because they think I'm your cousin. I don't want to rat the person out because I'm not calling to threaten or harm you in any way. I need help." His voice had a smooth quality, like warm cognac.

"I'm not sure I can help you, Mr. Newton. I'm in

the middle of a murder investigation, which is taking up valuable time," Kate said, then took another bite of her Butterfinger.

"That's just it. I can help you with that information. But I can't do it over the phone. You could record it or tap the line. Can we meet?" The desperation in his voice made her even more curious.

"In a public place? Because I'm not meeting you alone anywhere," Kate said.

"Sure, but it's got to be just you. I'd appreciate if you don't wear a recording device of any kind. But I can tell you who murdered Campbell and Foss."

Kate almost choked on her candy bar. "What about Lopez?"

"Him, too."

"Was it you?" she asked.

"Would I be calling you to implicate myself?"

"No, but you'd call to throw suspicion in another direction."

"I'll tell you this much, Campbell and Foss were killed because they stole from Payaso, but Payaso didn't kill Foss."

"How do you know this?" Kate pressed.

"I'll tell you when we meet."

"Fine, but a public place."

"And don't tell anyone. You have a mole in your department," Newton said.

His words hit Kate like a punch to the gut. Even the local drug dealers knew more about what was going on in the department than the brass. "Who?"

"I might just tell you that when we meet, too. Madison's on Main just after dark."

"Why not now?" Kate asked.

"I'm not in Peculiar right now. I'm taking care of some business. I'll see you around ten o'clock."

"How will I know you?" she asked.

"For real, lady? I have bright red hair. You can't miss me." He hung up.

Kate knew she shouldn't go alone, and especially not without telling anyone. But she planned to meet with Newton anyway, to see if he could really solve her case. She started her car and drove back to the station. She'd tell the chief.

"So what do you think?" Kate asked after giving all the information to her boss.

"I think you meet him. But you're not going alone. And you're going to arrive at least twenty minutes early. I want your backup to see him arrive after knowing you're in place."

"It's very public, so I don't see any problem with meeting him."

"Madison's isn't exactly in a good neighborhood. Make sure you're in uniform and turn on your chest camera as soon as you see him approach." Rambone shuffled through papers. "I need to make a call, get this situated. I'll have someone there, watching your back."

"But who can we trust? You said we have someone tipping these guys off. Maybe Newton is one of them.

Or he's the one getting the tips?" Kate leaned against the doorframe.

"We'll have to trust someone. Or maybe I'll just go myself. I'll keep an eye on you myself. I'll text you when I'm in place, so you know you have backup. Use your personal phone. No radios. We don't want to spook this guy."

Chapter 25

When Rambone said Madison's wasn't in a good area of town, he wasn't kidding. Peculiar didn't have many homeless people, but those who did sleep on the streets slept on the east side of Main Street, a few blocks from Madison's. The alleys were lined with cargo doors, the kind that roll up to uncover the actual entrance to the building beneath. The doors and walls were covered in graffiti. The visual just before dark felt surreal, like walking into a painting of many colors. Into someone's nightmare.

In full uniform, with one hand on her service weapon, Kate felt as safe as possible for the situation. She didn't expect anyone to come up to her panhandling, or to approach in anger. This side of town, the people kept to themselves. They didn't want to draw attention because they wanted to be invisible to society. Their rules, their ways, keep out.

Madison's, a local bar, looked like the type of place

you'd see in a movie. A long bar, with barstools pushed up close. A mirror behind the liquor on the wall. Only don't ask for Stoli in this bar, because they carried only well drinks. Their patrons didn't care what the label said, as long as the shit was strong and let them forget life for a little while.

Kate looked around the street. Only a handful of cars, one on blocks with the wheels removed and windows broken out. She sent a text to Rambone, then walked over and looked inside the 1980-something Monte Carlo. In the backseat, covered with just a thin sheet, she saw a body. She leaned in closer to make sure the person was still alive.

When the person (she couldn't tell if it was a man or woman, just that they stunk like rotten garbage) snorted and moved, Kate sucked in a breath and hit the back of her head as she backed away from the car. When she stepped back, she bumped into something. Make that someone.

She turned. "Payaso."

"Hello, Kate," he said in a heavy Mexican accent. Not his native accent, but the one the gangs had adopted.

Payaso wore a white "wife beater" tee, baggy jeans that fell just below his butt cheeks, baby blue boxers, a gold chain around his neck, and a slew of tattoos.

"How do you know my name?" Kate asked.

Before she registered what was going on, Payaso had his hand on her gun. She struggled to get free, and keep her gun at the same time. She twisted and pulled, then realized she needed to call in her position. Newton hadn't arrived, so she didn't have her chest camera on. Oh shit, all the things going through her head. The mistakes she'd made. She reached to arm her chest camera.

"Don't touch that," Payaso said, then yanked at her hip.

Payaso had her gun. Fuck.

"Come on, girl," he grabbed her upper arm and yanked.

I'm going to die, she thought. *Right here in the squalor of East Main Street, I'm going to die. Unless he takes me somewhere else.*

But he dragged her into the alley. She thought about screaming, but he had her gun.

Once in the shadows of the alley, Payaso pinned her against the wall. "I always wondered what a pig tasted like." He leaned in close and ran his tongue up her neck.

Kate struggled. Reaching for her radio, she moved slowly, trying to make the move seem natural. She had her finger on the button when Payaso ripped it from her reach, then threw it down the alley. That cut off the connection to the mic at her shoulder. Kate gasped. She hoped dispatch would realize it was her radio, and find the location of her vehicle.

"Lots of layers," Payaso said. He reached up and unbuttoned her shirt, but only the first two or three before he got impatient and tore the rest of her shirt away. "Fuckin' eh."

"What are you doing? Just let me go." Kate didn't beg, she used all the authority she could muster in her voice.

He put the gun to her temple. "Shut the fuck up before I blow your head off and fuck your corpse." He slammed the gun into the side of her head.

Kate stopped talking. She stopped breathing. Everything got swirly, then went black.

She couldn't have been out too long, but when she came to, Payaso had her stripped down to her bra and panties, straddling her as she lay on the filth of the concrete alley.

She started to say something, then decided to keep quiet. Payaso ran the gun up her torso, the metal cold against her hot skin. Even though the temperature had dropped to the eighties, she felt sweat on her brow, between her breasts, and at the small of her back. Was it heat or terror making her sweat? Eighty wasn't hot. And the concrete even felt a little cool.

Still groggy from the impact, Kate knew her predicament. If she didn't get away, didn't get her gun back, Payaso was going to rape her. After all she'd been through, this was how it ended. Because no way he was letting her live. She went limp, trying not to feel his skin on her skin, his tongue on her belly. She fought to find a way to get out from under him, then decided she wasn't going down without a fucking fight.

Payaso had her hands down at her sides, his knees holding them just under her hips. She bucked hard, moving his scrawny body just enough to get a hand

231

loose. She shoved at him, trying to free her other hand. She had to get that gun away from him. Crazy things crossed her mind: she would not be killed with her own service weapon. He might rape her, but she'd never let him kill her with her own gun.

Payaso smacked her hard in the face, but this time it didn't knock her out.

The white-hot pain shot across her cheekbone, and she felt her nose crack, then felt the blood running down onto her lips into her mouth. "Fuck you, asshole. You're not taking me down like this." She twisted her body to the left.

Payaso didn't move an inch. He sat down hard and fast on her hips. "You stupid fucking pig. Just sit still." He leaned over and the full weight of his body covered her. She could feel his chest against hers, and she couldn't stop the feeling inside. She felt ill, embarrassed, fucking pissed off. And not pissed off at Payaso, but at herself. She was stronger than this. But he had her down, and had her hands above her head now. She could struggle all she wanted, but he'd do it, and she couldn't stop him.

He let go of her right hand, his right hand holding the gun and her left hand. He rounded his back, and reached between them, feeling for the zipper of his pants. That's when Kate felt his erection, and her stomach lurched. She projectile vomited into the air, and all over the front of Payaso.

He flew up off her, but still sat on her hips, his erection protruding from his unzipped jeans. "Fucking bitch!" The gun in his hand aimed at her face.

"Oscar," she heard a voice from behind her.

Payaso looked up.

Kate braced for the blow as she choked on her own vomit. But instead of a blow, she heard the concussion of gunfire as it echoed off the walls of the alley.

This time, Payaso bucked and fell back. Kate saw the gun drop from his hand.

She struggled to sit up, and crawled across the filth to grab the gun, but Payaso's hand got there first. He wrapped his fingers around the grip and fired. It was Kate's turn to fall back, but even with the burning pain searing her belly, she ripped the gun from Payaso's hand. He'd lost all strength and didn't even fight her.

She pushed to get to her knees, her legs in a tangle, then using the wall, she got to her feet. Then she aimed her gun at Payaso's head and emptied her magazine. She heard breathing behind her and expected to see her boss finally catching up to what had happened.

Instead, she saw a tall thin man with orange hair, his gun still aimed at Payaso.

Kate sucked in a short breath. "You...asshole...you set...me up."

Newton stepped forward. "No, I didn't. I came here to tell you, Payaso and Vega killed Lopez. Payaso wanted it all. Lopez had the weed business, but Payaso had his own. Lopez stepped on the wrong toes."

Kate could barely register his words. "Call 911."

"I called before I came down the alley. I heard

Payaso. I had no idea you were, well, naked, until I came around the corner." Newton's voice oozed concern. "I'm so sorry. I should have told you over the phone. I'm so sorry." Newton helped Kate into a sitting position against the wall, then stepped back.

"What about Kim?" Kate managed to whisper. She looked up, but Newton was gone. Then everything was gone.

As Kate slowly faded, she realized, even though she fought, she'd still die by her own gun. *Damn it, this sucks,* was her final thought before everything went blank.

Chapter 26

By the time Zane found out Kate had been shot, she was already in surgery. Racing, Code 3 (lights and siren), he ran into the hospital emergency area just in time to see Bryce coming out of the elevator.

"Where is she?" Zane asked.

"Where is who?" Bryce cocked his head, frowning at Zane's frantic demeanor.

"Kate. She was shot." Zane said a little too loud.

"Oh, shit, no. Hold on." Bryce went behind the nurse's station and looked in the computer, then at paperwork on a clipboard.

Zane followed him to the desk. "Well?"

"She's in surgery," Bryce said. "That's all I know at this point. Let me see what else I can find out."

Zane watched Bryce calmly jog to the secured doors, swipe his employee pass, and disappear as the doors closed behind him.

"Zane," Jake called from the waiting area of the ER.

"Hey, what do you know?" Zane asked, grasping Jake's shoulders.

"I was with the captain when we got the call. She was found in an alley next to Madison's. It was so dirty and dark, like something out of a dark thriller movie. Two bodies. One on the ground and the other slumped against the wall." Jake looked off like he was seeing it all again for the first time.

"The other body? Who was it?" Zane asked.

"Oscar Silva. They called him Payaso," Jake said.

"Is he the one who shot Kate?"

Jake shrugged. "We don't know much right now. Just that Kate was gut shot, and someone emptied a magazine on Payaso."

"He's dead?" Zane tensed as he felt the need for the loser to be dead.

"Oh, yeah, dead for sure."

"And Kate? What about her?"

"We found her wearing only a bra and underwear, and her underwear had been pulled down, or slipped down, I don't know, but they were close to her knees. Her uniform had been taken off and pieces spread down the alley. Captain Francois thinks Payaso undressed her as he walked her deep into the alley."

"Did the call come from Madison's? They heard the gunshots?" He didn't want to hear any more about Kate's state of undress. It made him want to vomit.

"No, the call came from a burner cell phone."

Captain Ollie Francois walked up. He wore his patrol uniform, and looked as put together as a man in an expensive suit. He stood the same height as Zane, and kept his silver hair cropped close. His Roman nose cast a shadow over his thin lips.

"Zane, you need to go home. We'll call you when we know more," Captain Francois said.

"I'm not going anywhere. That's my officer, and my ex-wife. And I want to know why the hell she was in East Peculiar at that time of night in uniform! She was off duty at six." Zane's fists clenched as he tried to hold his temper in check.

"Look, I don't know. Maybe she went to Madison's after work for a drink," Francois said.

"No, she'd go home, or to my pop's place. No way she'd be in uniform on that side of town if she wasn't working. And now she's in surgery and no one can tell me her condition. Did you even speak to her at the scene?"

Ollie shook his head. "She was unconscious and unresponsive when we found her. I'm sorry."

"And that filthy piece of garbage, Payaso, he raped her?" Zane willed the tears of anger and frustration away.

"It doesn't appear she was raped," Jake said.

Zane breathed deep. *Thank God.*

He paced the hallway, not wanting to talk to Francois and Underwood. He turned his head every time he heard a door, looking for Bryce. Maybe he'd have more answers. He looked at his watch and time seemed to move in slow motion. He'd heard about this, but he'd never experienced the clock moving so slow.

"Zane," Bryce said, coming up behind him.

"Bryce. What do you know?" Zane stopped pacing.

"She's in surgery, they will probably be another hour or so. She was shot in the stomach. And it looks like she was beat up pretty bad. The nurse I spoke to said her face was bloody and swollen, and it looked like she might have had her nose broken. She couldn't be sure because of the swelling."

Zane stopped breathing. His girl was hurt and he couldn't do a damn thing. He never felt so helpless in his life. "What about recovery time?"

"I don't know right now, but I'd guess she'll be hospitalized for several days, then she'll need months to recover." Bryce's voice calm and passive. "Look, I'm moving out to the house with her, so I'll keep an eye on her."

"But the bedroom is upstairs. She can't be walking up and down those stairs," Zane said. "She can come stay with me."

"That's not going to happen and you know it. I'll get something set up on the first floor. Lord knows there are plenty of rooms downstairs. And there's a servant's quarters off the kitchen. I can get that fixed up for her before she gets home."

Zane shook his head. "She needs to be closer to the hospital."

Bryce put his hand on Zane's shoulder. "Look, man, I know you love her, but she can't and won't stay with you. She'll probably barely tolerate you visiting. You know how she is. She'll let me dote on her because I'm her brother, and she'll bitch about that."

"But you have to work. Who will watch her? I mean, it looks like she killed a gangbanger. And not a low level one, either. They'll come after her. She can't be alone."

"She won't be. I promise. We can work out a schedule."

Zane's legs quivered, and he barely made it to the chair before collapsing. "What if she dies?"

Bryce walked to the chair. Standing over Zane like a behemoth, he said, "Stop that stupid talk. I've got to get back to work, but as soon as I know more, I'll call you. Okay?"

Zane didn't even look up, his head in his hands. "I just don't understand. Why was she even near Madison's?"

"Madison's? That's where they found her?" Bryce stopped walking away and turned back to Zane.

"Yes, in the alley behind Madison's. Do you have any idea why she'd go there?" Zane stared up at Bryce now.

"That's insane. She wouldn't go there. Not alone." Bryce balled up his fists. "Something stinks, Zane. I mean really stinks. But I've got to go. I'll call you if I hear anything, I promise. The doctor and nurses know you're here, so you might hear from them before I do."

Zane slumped down in the chair, then jumped up. "Captain!"

Francois walked into the seating area, meeting Zane halfway. "What's up?"

"Tell me everything you know. And where the hell is the chief?"

"I just got off the phone with him. He's on his way."

"He should have been here," Zane said.

"He's coming. He said he got tied up with business."

Zane's face reddened. "What do you know? I mean the smallest detail."

Francois told them about the call. They were closest when Dispatch sent out the call. When he checked back, the call had come from a burner cell, so they couldn't trace it. They might be able to with further investigation, but it wasn't going to be quick and easy. She'd been beat up, and even though she was nearly naked, she wasn't raped. Payaso would be at the morgue shortly and they'd expedite the autopsy. Somebody, most likely Kate, unloaded her full magazine on Payaso. Weirdly, one shot to the torso, and the rest to his face and neck. Blood everywhere in the alley.

"Look, we don't know why she was there. I asked the chief when I talked to him, and he said he didn't know, either. Darby had clocked out at six almost on the dot," Francois finished.

"Hopefully she remembers more when she's out of

surgery." He put his face in his hands again. "I just can't lose her."

"She's gonna make it." Francois patted Zane's shoulder.

Zane paced the waiting area for another hour before the doctor came out and asked for him. Dressed in scrubs, with the face mask around his neck and his Looney Tunes cap still on his head, he reached out to shake Zane's hand.

"I'm Dr. Mollenstad. I performed the surgery on your ex-wife. She's out of surgery and doing well, considering. The bullet didn't hit any major organs or arteries. Her face is a little banged up, too. Broken cheekbone and we reset her nose. She looks really bad right now. The damage to her face could be a lot worse."

Zane took a deep breath. "She's okay," he said more to himself than anyone.

"She is. It will be a while until she comes out of the anesthesia fully, but you're welcome to come sit in her room as soon as they release her."

"Yes, I'd like that," Zane said.

"I'll have my nurse come get you when Ms. Darby is in a room." He shook Zane's hand again.

Zane sat down, exhausted from worry, then looked up to see Kate's adoptive parents walk through the door. He stood. "Mr. and Mrs. Darby."

"Bryce called us. We got here as soon as we could." They all embraced in a hug.

Zane caught them up on the details, letting them know she'd be okay.

Mr. Darby said, "Physically, but what about mentally?"

The thought had crossed Zane's mind. He didn't know the answer to that one.

Chapter 27

Zane sat in the room with the Darbys and Bryce for a couple of hours. Kate slept the entire time. About three in the morning, Bryce left with his parents to get them set up in a hotel, and Zane fell asleep. He woke up at 4:13 and looked over to Kate lying in the bed, hooked up to at least three different machines. He swore he saw her eyelids move a little and jumped up to be by her side.

Holding her limp hand, Zane leaned over to kiss it when he heard, "Zane?"

He looked up at Kate's face, looking closely for the first time. It hurt his entire body to look at her battered and bruised face, swollen eyes, and stitches on her temple. "I'm here, babe, I'm here."

She squeezed his hand, but it was so weak, it was barely finger movement.

"So tired," she said.

"Don't talk. Just rest. You have plenty of time. Go back to sleep." He patted the top of her hand.

"Ncnnn," Kate said.

Zane leaned down closer to her face, as her voice came out light and weak. "What did you say?"

She mumbled something that sounded like, "Find Newton."

To be sure, he said, "Did you say, 'Find Newton?'"

She wiggled her fingers, then fell back to sleep.

Zane sat in the chair, stewing over Kate's words. *"Find Newton."* Weren't they already looking for the guy? Did he have something to do with the murders on M Street? Zane felt himself start to burn from his core. Or did Newton do this?

Bryce returned to Kate's room around five-thirty, and Zane got up to go to the bathroom, using the one in Kate's room. Then he excused himself and went out into the hallway. Zane and Kate's family had decided she'd have no visitors for the night, so Francois and Underwood hadn't seen Kate yet.

Zane pulled out his phone and sent Jake a text: *Come to the hospital when you finish your shift.*

Jake responded immediately: *I'll be there in less than an hour.*

Zane didn't know who he could trust, but decided Jake was still too new to be corrupted. He didn't know enough people to have made friends or pick up any informants he owed. And Zane needed an ally. He couldn't do this himself. He needed to find Newton. And Jake might be able to find out from Kim where

Newton could be found. It was a long shot, but worth a try. He couldn't tell anyone else, because he was sure someone had sent Payaso after Kate, and he had no idea who.

True to his word, Jake arrived in less than an hour. "How is she doing?" were the first words out of his mouth.

"She'll live, but it's going to be a long road. She's pretty beat up."

Jake looked at the floor of the hospital hallway. "I know. It was hard to look at her last night. I imagine the swelling is worse now."

"Broken cheekbone and nose. Her eyes are black, and her eyeballs, what I could see of them, looked blood red. She's gonna hurt pretty bad once the surgery meds wear off. I hope the morphine is enough. But that's not why I called you."

"What's going on?"

"Kate said Geo Newton's name. She said to find him. Did you or Francois hear anything about Newton and what happened with Kate last night?" Zane's face creased with concern and longing to know the answers.

"The captain and I went back to the scene after we left the hospital. Chief Rambone wanted us to get a second look at the crime scene. Nothing was mentioned about Newton at all. Isn't he a person of interest in the M Street murders?" Jake shoved his hands into the pockets of the pullover hoodie he wore over his uniform.

"He is. And I need to find him. If he's the one who shot Kate, I'll kill him myself."

"That doesn't seem right, Sergeant Gwilly. From everything at the scene, it looks like Silva ambushed Darby and dragged her into the alley. Somehow, he got the better of her, undressing her. From the evidence, Silva tried to rape her, but someone shot him before he could succeed. It could have been Kate, but from the dirt on her back, he had her on the ground. Silva had grease and dirt on his knees. So maybe he straddled Kate, but the angle of the bullet doesn't make sense."

"In what way doesn't it make sense?" Zane asked, wanting to shake Jake to get him to the point faster.

"No way could Kate have shot him while lying on the ground. He was shot straight on. It's obvious from the exit wound. Straight in and out. Not an angle."

"What did Chief Rambone say?" Zane asked.

"He thinks I need to keep close to Kim. She knows more than she's letting on."

"That's not exactly what I meant, but that will do. Let's go have a chat with Kim."

"She's still in County. No one bailed her out this time."

Zane didn't have time for any crap, and he made sure the jailer understood. Kim hadn't even had breakfast yet when they escorted her into the interview room.

"You?" Kim immediately turned back to the jailer. "I have no desire to talk to these assholes."

The jailer looked at Zane, then back at Kim. "Sit down. Listen to what they have to say."

Kim rocked her head from side to side, then turned and said, "What do you want with me?"

Zane and Jake sat down, Kim followed suit.

"I'm sure you know your boyfriend was killed," Jake said.

Kim frowned. "Foss?" She showed no emotion.

"Silva," Zane said.

Kim's frown deepened. "Silva?"

Jake leaned closer. "Payaso."

Kim's frown fell away, her cool demeanor crumbled. "That's not even funny."

"He's not kidding," Zane said.

Kim's entire body shook like an addict coming off a three-day high. Tears rolled down her cheeks. She took deep, sobbing breaths, but didn't make any sound.

Smug, Jake said, "No one is coming to save you now, Kim. No one."

"Fuck you, Jake. As usual, you don't know anything." She spat the words literally, spittle flying through the air, rolling down her chin.

"You're right, he doesn't know shit, but you do," Zane said.

Jake looked at Zane as if he'd been thrown under a bus. Zane couldn't look at him, for fear of losing his character.

"I don't know anything. If I did, I'd be able to get out of here. Isn't that what you always want, information? 'I'll cut you a deal for the right information,' isn't that how it always goes?" Kim rocked in her chair, the tears still streaming down her face.

"How did Andy Foss die?" Jake asked.

She turned on him. "Isn't that your job to figure out?"

"I have a theory," Zane said. "My theory goes something like this. You were at that house the night Foss was killed."

"Duh! You already knew that."

"Kim, they found GSR on your clothes. And the residue matches the residue on the back of Foss's head."

Kim shook her head hard. "No, no, no."

"Yes. You shot Andy Foss, didn't you?"

"Is that why you're trying to say Payaso is dead, so I'll turn on him, then you'll arrest him and use me as a witness? Well, you can shove that up your ass, because I'm married to him. I can't testify."

You could have heard a tear drop in the room as Jake's eyes went wide and his mouth opened a little. Zane and Jake glanced at each other, neither believing her.

"This isn't a joke Kim. Payaso is dead. I'll bring photos if that's what you want." Then a thought came to him. "We're looking for his killer."

Zane planned to look at the county records to see if Kim was bluffing about being married to Payaso. But for now, he had other, more important issues.

"It don't matter who killed him. They don't need you doling out justice. They'll dole out their own brand. And it won't be all prettied up with a judge and jury. Whoever killed my man will die an ugly, gruesome death, I promise you." She continued to rock, her body now rigid. "I'll get out of here, and I'll make sure of it."

By they, Zane knew she spoke of the Nazar cartel. Payaso had been untouchable because of his connections and rank in the cartel. Payaso planned his own death when he took on Kate. Or had he? How did he know Kate would be there? And why was she there in the first place? He couldn't stop running the questions in his mind.

"Kim, you're never getting out. Murder one is on the table now. But what I don't understand is why you killed Andy."

"You're crazy. No way you're pinning that on me. Maybe I was standing next to the person killed him. Wasn't me." Defiant, yet the look in her eyes screamed, "I'm terrified."

Jake cut to the chase. "Tell us the truth about Geo Newton. He wasn't your boyfriend, obviously. But you know him. I know he was working the area the night of the raid. Did he tip you off? Was that why we didn't find any drugs in that house?"

"Fuck Newton, he's a nobody." Kim stopped rocking. They had her attention.

Zane waited a beat, looking closely as Kim's eyes darted back and forth at warp speed between Jake and him. She was coming down hard. How many days had it been? Zane was too tired to count.

"What do you know about Newton?" Jake asked.

"I know he's a snitch. He's a goody goody, driving around in his Range Rover with his fancy clothes. Thinks he's too good."

"Do you know where he hangs out?" Zane asked.

Kim glared at him. "How the fuck should I know?"

Zane felt something missing in Kim's words. He pondered her words one more time. What was it? Then he almost slapped the table with his hand. Venom. Her words lacked venom. She knew more than she let on.

"We think Newton killed Payaso," Zane said.

Kim completely crumbled. Her back rolled forward, and she dropped her head to her knees, her arms hanging limp, with her cuffed wrists still in her lap. She no longer shook, but took long, controlled breaths. When she looked back up, she said, "His aunt lives on River Drive. When he's in town he stays with her sometimes."

"Do you know the address?" Zane asked.

She looked up. "I don't, but it's a yellow house. Not bright yellow, but like the color of the inside of a banana."

They'd hit a nerve. If Newton killed Payaso, she wanted him to pay. She wanted them to find him. And Zane always thought the inside of a banana was more of a cream color, certainly not yellow. But whatever. They'd find the house.

They stood.

"Two more things. The first one: why did you hesitate before you pulled the trigger when you shot Foss?" Zane asked coolly, as if asking her favorite color.

Kim sat up straight, staring Zane down. She said nothing.

"Okay, if that's how you want to play it, all the details will come out at the trial." He turned to leave.

"I thought you said two things," Kim goaded him.

Jake stood at the door, waiting for the jailer to buzz them out. Zane turned back to Kim. "Oh, yeah, Newton didn't kill Payaso. Your *husband* tried to rape Corporal Darby, and she unloaded her gun on him. Payaso was killed by the cops."

As they walked out the door, Kim screamed, "I'm gonna kill that bitch when I get out of here."

Chapter 28

They didn't need to look for a banana yellow house. As Zane drove to River Drive, Jake looked up all known addresses for Geo Newton. "19873 River Drive."

Zane pushed a little harder on the accelerator, but he didn't want to speed through town. They didn't need any mistakes. He needed to talk to Newton. Kill him if need be, because he wouldn't be giving this guy a way out. Not if he was in any way involved in what happened to Kate.

"Do we just go up and knock on the door?" Jake asked.

Zane nodded his head to the front porch of the yellow house, which Zane would have called cream, not yellow. A young man with bright red hair sat on a wooden rocker, rocking and staring at them.

"It's about time," Newton said, and stopped rocking.

"You want to talk here?" Zane asked.

"My aunt is at work. Let's go inside." Newton opened the screen door and walked inside.

The solid door remained open, so Newton never left their field of view. Zane followed him in the house, feeling safe. No way Newton was armed. He wore only boxer shorts and a fitted tee against his tight frame.

Newton sat in an upholstered chair and indicated the couch for Jake and Zane. "How is Officer Darby?"

Zane immediate stiffened. "What do you know about Corporal Darby?"

"I called it in." He hung his head. "Man, I'm sorry. No one was supposed to know she'd be there. I wanted to give her information, but I couldn't do it over the phone. I had no idea she'd be followed."

"What are you talking about?" Zane asked.

"I called Darby on her cell. Don't ask how I got the number, cuz I'm not going to tell you. I told her I knew some things, but I couldn't tell her on the phone. I didn't know who might be listening. We planned to meet at Madison's. Neutral ground and all. Then I ditched my phone, in case the cops were tracing it. I got a burner phone. We were supposed to meet at like ten or so. She musta got there early. I heard a noise in the alley as I walked from the parking lot to Madison's, and that's when I saw Payaso straddling Darby. He held her hands and a gun, and was pushing his jeans down when I walked up."

"Did he rape her?" Zane asked, wondering if the police were wrong.

"No, man. I'd just pulled my gun and Payaso sat up.

I think Darby puked on him. At least it smelled really bad like vomit. I called his name, and when he looked away from the cop and at me, I shot him in the chest. Darby scrambled up, grabbing for Payaso's gun, but he somehow grabbed it from the ground before she could get it. He shot her. As she fell back, she grabbed for the gun, and Payaso must have been almost dead, because he just let go. She had a bit of trouble, but she got to her knees, stood right over him, and emptied her magazine. She thought I set her up. I didn't, man. I didn't. Anyway, I called 911 and got the hell out of Dodge."

Zane sighed with relief. Kate was absolutely not raped. But he knew she'd feel raped of her dignity for getting caught off guard. She never would have been in that situation had she been more careful, or at least she'd see it that way. "Why did she think you set her up?"

Newton threw his hands up. "It was just me and her, man. I didn't tell nobody I was meeting her. She promised to come alone."

"I talked to her captain and the chief, and they both said they had no idea why she was there," Zane said. "How would Payaso know? Do you think he'd been following her?"

"Could be, I don't know. Me and Payaso ain't exactly friends, you know. We used to be, but his loyalty to the gang life, well, we just ain't friends now."

"What were you going to tell Darby?" Jake asked, sounding anxious.

"Look, there was 'bout to be an all-out turf war.

254

Lopez stepped on some toes, and Payaso took him out. Payaso said he didn't want none of that weed Lopez was peddling, and Lopez showed up anyway. Him and Danny Boyd been going around to the usual haunts. Payaso took him out."

"Did Boyd know Payaso killed Lopez?" Zane asked.

"That I don't know. But I know Danny's big mouth is what got Lopez in the hurt in the first place. Danny accidentally talked too much. But that's just Danny. And that's not all. Fuckin' Danny, he told Payaso that the Kim Vega chick was blowing Foss for drugs. And that didn't even make sense, because Payaso kept her hooked up."

"So Payaso knew Kim had hooked up with Foss? And by hooked up, I'm talking sex, not drugs," Jake said.

"One and the same, sex for drugs, you know?" Newton said. "And it all went to shit from there. Next thing I know, Nazar's people are looking for me, and Payaso is looking for a fall guy."

"You?" Zane asked.

"I guess so. But I wasn't waiting around to find out. That's why I called Darby. I heard she was the cop investigating the murders. Personally, I feel bad for Leon, man, he was in the wrong place at the wrong time. Ain't no reason to kill poor Leon. He's a good guy."

"But Leon was in the house, so he got killed. Do you know who killed him?" Zane asked.

"I wasn't there, and this is second hand, but I

heard, Payaso walked in with Kim, and saw Foss OD'ed at the kitchen table. Payaso picked Andy up by the hair, and handed the gun to Kim. Made her put the gun to Foss's head and pull the trigger. But I wasn't there, so that's just the story I heard. Then they heard noise upstairs and Payaso ran up the stairs and killed poor Leon."

Yeah, yeah, poor, doped up Leon, Zane thought. "So who's pedaling the fentanyl?"

"I actually think Payaso's crew put that on the streets. He said something about a bad load of shit he got and instead of cutting it, he was selling full strength just to get rid of it."

"I thought you weren't friends?" Jake said.

"We ain't, but I ain't stupid, I got my guys on the inside. Just like he got his guys watching me."

"So do you think that's how he knew you were meeting with Darby?" Zane asked.

Newton shook his head. "No way no one knew, but Darby and me, unless she told someone. And I told her not to tell no one."

"Someone knew. Again, maybe Payaso followed her. I don't know."

"So should you read me my rights?" Newton asked, putting his wrists together as if ready to be cuffed.

"Look, I don't have anything on you. I can't put you at the scene, but someone is going to be looking for the gun that shot that bullet into Payaso's chest."

"I know. I'm willing to go without a fight. I'm going

to die either here or on the inside when Nazar's people find out I shot Payaso." He stood.

"Right now, only Jake and I know what you did. There's no reason to make a federal case out of it. We'll get back to you when the time is right, but no one's going to prison for the murders of Lopez, Foss, and Campbell, because Silva is dead. Right now, nothing comes back to you."

Newton walked them to the door. "Hey, I'm really sorry about the lady cop. I ain't never shot no one until last night. And I sure wouldn't shoot a cop. I know I'm a criminal, but other than a few misdemeanors, I don't have a record. Hell, I ain't even a felon. I could carry a registered gun if I wanted."

Zane chuckled at Newton's cockiness. "Thanks for talking to us. Maybe next time you can offer us some sweet tea."

As they walked down the steps, Jake said, "I hate sweet tea."

Epilogue

About an hour after Zane and Jake left Geo's aunt's house, there was a knock at the door. Geo looked through the window and didn't hesitate to open the door. Swinging the door wide, he said, "Did you have more questions?"

The gun came up before Geo could bolt. The last thing he saw before he saw the ceiling in his aunt's house was the end of the silencer. He lay on the floor, staring at the water stains on the ceiling, thinking he should talk to his aunt about having the roof repaired. Then he thought about nothing at all.

If you enjoyed reading this novel, I would appreciate it if you would help others enjoy the book, too.

Review it. Please tell others why you liked this book by reviewing it on the site where you purchased the book, on your favorite book site, or on your blog.

Lend it. This eBook is lending-enabled, so please feel free to share with a friend.

Recommend it. Please help other readers find the book by recommending it to readers' groups, discussion boards, Goodreads, etc.

Email me. I'd love to hear from you jamie@jamieleescott.com http://www.jamieleescott.com

Website: http://www.jamieleescott.com
Twitter http://www.twitter.com/authorjamie
Facebook Fan Page:
http://www.facebook.com/authorjamie
Be a part of the Clues Crew and get a sneak peek at works in progress
and join the fun and giveaways.
https://www.facebook.com/groups/jamiescluecrew/

Want to be the first to read Jamie Lee Scott know about new releases, get advanced sneak peeks at new novels, and fun giveaways?

Subscribe to Jamie's newsletter for
EXCLUSIVE novella ebook
HOMICIDE, LIFE WITH NICK
So if you're not a newsletter subscriber, here's your chance.
This is open to international readers too.
*must be deliverable online

Click here to get the newsletter!

Other books by Jamie Lee Scott

<u>Kate Darby Series</u>

Angry Betty

Bang Switch

Check Six

Dirty Bite

Electric Slide

<u>Gotcha Detective Agency Mystery Series</u>

Let Us Prey

Textual Relations

Death of a Sales Rep

What a Meth

Tagged You're It (a novelette)

Bad Vice

Electile Dysfunction

Who Gives A Split

Mary Had a Little Scam

Trespassers Will be Prostituted

The Knife Before Christmas

A Lie in Every Truth

Love is a Many Splintered Thing

Claus Trophobic

Willa Friday Culinary Cozy Mystery Series

A Thyme to Die

Keto Can Kill You

Tainted Tiramisu

Avocado Toasted

Made in the USA
Las Vegas, NV
02 August 2022

52561437R00163